The HOTEL MARCEL

DINING CLUB

BY INVITATION ONLY

A Small Volume For Lovers of *HAUTE CUISINE*

Elizabeth Cooke

abbott press

This is a work of fiction. All of the characters, names, incidents, organizations, and dialogue in this novel are either the products of the author's imagination or are used fictitiously.

Abbott Press books may be ordered through booksellers or by contacting:

Abbott Press
1663 Liberty Drive
Bloomington, IN 47403
www.abbottpress.com
Phone: 1 (866) 697-5310

Cover design by Todd Engel

ISBN: 978-1-4582-2019-6 (sc)
ISBN: 978-1-4582-2018-9 (hc)
ISBN: 978-1-4582-2017-2 (e)

Library of Congress Control Number: 2016905622

Print information available on the last page.

Abbott Press rev. date: 05/10/2016

PROLOGUE

Paris
Cuisine
The two are synonymous.

ON THIS VISIT to the Hotel Marcel, I find myself in a food fight! It becomes a contest intense enough to perhaps make one sick. Or worse.

Yet, food is the sustenance of love, and the delightful embellishments that come from exquisite *entremets* leave little to be desired.

Food. Such a dull word! But how important it is; it supports survival, yes, but is also the essence of love. It not only nurtures the baby at the breast, it feeds the spirit as one grows, and when one is of age, the enormity of food choices and delights to the tongue, give life a particular squeeze of pleasure. No doubt!

Is food a panacea? A remedy for all ills? In many ways, yes. How important and intense is the food connection to emotions and experience! In sadness. When deprived. In love. In sickness. After hurting someone deeply, that gaping hole of remorse. And anger! The need to crunch one's teeth and gnaw on the offender.

Awaiting a trial, a lover's call, a birth. One consoles oneself with constant nibbles to make the minutes fly and keep one from biting one's nails.

And there is celebration. Or depression, after great loss - of money – love – death. A plethora of sweets and chocolate is the answer. In exuberance and elation? What else but *champagne* and caviar, lobster and liqueurs! Ah, the Final Supper.

I am in Paris once more, the city of dreams. I will find my visit (I try to come here at least every six months) will have a totally different flavor from any previous sojourns.

And those flavors, the coloration, the experience of French *cuisine* become an adventurous story unto itself.

Bon Appétit!!

CHAPTER 1

Hotel Marcel

L'AUTOMNE! PARIS! BRIT!

It is a glorious, sunny Saturday morning, this 24th of October, when I arrive at Charles de Gaulle airport. It has been almost a year since I have been in the city I love so much.

Brit, my artist/lover/friend is there to greet me with his old Peugeot. At least he was able to stay with me on Long Island for almost six weeks, early last summer, a time of play and love and some spectacular paintings.

How I have missed him! But I am close again to him now, and happily clamber into the car. Before buckling myself to safety, we embrace passionately.

"You're here," he breathes, into my hair.

"You bet I am," I whisper back.

Releasing me, he starts the car and drives me to my small hotel: Hotel Marcel. The back of his Peugeot has several crated paintings, as he is on his way to the gallery on the right bank, to drop them off at Fernand et Fils, after he leaves me. The gallery is to exhibit his works in a few weeks. My baggage – one large and one carry-on – are also stuffed in the rear of the car.

At the entrance of the hotel, he stops, rounds the front of the car to open my door (very gentlemanly!) and I disembark. Brit brings my suitcase to the hotel stoop, as I clutch the carry-on. We embrace, there, in the strong morning sunlight. He runs off with a final little wave, and the words, "See you tonight. I can't wait!" and, with a kiss, I enter the foyer.

Willie Blakely is at the front desk. "Madame Elizabeth," he says with a big grin and comes forward to collect my suitcase. I touch his shoulder. "Ah, Willie," I say. "How good to see you and how good to be back."

"We been awaiting you, Madame, with much impatience." His cockney accent is as strong as ever.

"And Jean-Luc?" I inquire.

"In his office, Madame."

Brigitte, the young *femme à tout faire* is in the salon, smiling, ready to serve me the breakfast of *café/croissant*, yogurt, and fruit juice. This repast is produced every morning, from the tiny kitchen at the back of the salon. It is the only food service provided by the hotel.

"Not right now, Brigitte, but thank you," I call to her. "Such a warm welcome," I exclaim to the two, as I make my way, with my carry-on, to the decrepit *ascenseur* at the rear of the building. As I say this, I hear a loud crash, as if a wall has crumbled to the floor. There is also the sound of breaking glass, then a loud shriek *"Dieu!"* This noise is followed by two male voices raised in anger rising to a high crescendo. The curse words fly, in rapid French (I know enough of the language to realize the viciousness and threat they imply), but also in English.

Willie is frozen in place, my suitcase in hand. He drops it and both of us run down the narrow hall to Jean-Luc's office door, behind which the insults continue to escalate.

Willie taps on the door, "Monsieur Marcel. Monsieur Marcel." Then louder, "Jean-Luc!" Tap, tap, tap.

I move from behind and start to pound on the door. "Jean-Luc! *C'est moi*. Madame Elizabeth."

There is silence on the other side of the door. A deathly silence - no sound - the two outside the door – Willie and me – and those inside the office – Jean-Luc and who? We are immobilized and mute. This lasts for what seems like many minutes, when suddenly the door flies open.

CHAPTER 2

Fisticuffs?

I SEE A furious Jean-Luc, red in the face, behind his desk. On the floor is broken glass, and in the corner, near where the armoire containing china and ceramic figurines of hotel bellboys that Jean-Luc has collected from all over the world – his treasured hobby – where the armoire had once stood – there is a blank wall.

The wall is slightly stained, and the armoire, which had stood against it is upon the floor, glass doors in shards and the china bellboys scattered in pieces from one end of the office to the other.

Next to that wall is, of all people - Nelson from the Majestic, the grand hotel directly next door! He is standing with his chest out and his cheeks puffed up, arms akimbo.

The fight is all about food!

Nelson, apparently, appears in Jean-Luc's office near 10:00 AM, earlier this Saturday morning. His visit is unexpected and of course, the hotelier is polite, though cool, in receiving the Manager of The Maj! Nelson is not the head Manager, but a *sous* Manager, stationed at the front desk, a troubleshooter for minor infractions within the hotel and among the guests.

And trouble there is! The trouble, apparently, is the Hotel Marcel!

According to Nelson, the *Fusion* dining room at The Maj is experiencing a sharp decline in customers.

"This cannot be because of the excellent Japanese *chef* the hotel employs. He is famous for his sushi and his exotic combinations…" Nelson is expounding.

"*Eh bien*, many of us have found his concoctions…well…not all that impressive…" Jean-Luc interjects.

"That's ridiculous. Atari – that's his name - is famous, not only in Japan, but he has worked as head *chef* at the Plaza Hotel in New York City…"

"I don't care where he's worked…" Jean-Luc says, rising from his desk. "His food is – how you say it in English – his food is lousy."

"There! This is exactly the problem!" Nelson is shouting. "You and your…people…you are bad mouthing the dining room. Even when you come in - you are smirking and rude…very offensive." Nelson lowers his voice. "You must be careful, Monsieur Marcel. You could be in for a lawsuit." His tone is threatening.

Jean-Luc bursts out laughing. "You must be making a joke." He can hardly contain his chuckles.

"And how about that American woman you brought to the dining room last year! Her credit card was unacceptable. No good! That's the kind of person you cater to in this lamentable hotel – if you can call it a hotel. Look at this cluttered office. It's disgusting."

(Of course, he was referring to last years' 'identity theft' that I lived through, a vindictive woman trying to embarrass me. She had cancelled my credit card, which of course, I did not know at the time. It resulted in *Fusion* refusing it.)

"Now, just a minute, you *bâtard!*" Jean-Luc, now outraged, shouts.

"You call me …" and the cursing begins in earnest. According to Jean-Luc later, the two men are nose to nose at one point, ready to share blows,

Elizabeth Cooke

but, instead, Nelson whirls around and grabs the edge of the armoire with its china bellboys, and with a great thrust, hurls it to the ground.

Jean-Luc is standing there in horror, furious, when the tapping on the door occurs, then my pounding. It is actually Nelson who flings open the door.

CHAPTER 3

The Broken Bellboys

ALL FOUR OF us – Willie, Jean-Luc, Nelson, myself – we all stand there stupefied, looking one to the other. Then, as Jean-Luc moves forward, his face twisted in anguish over the loss of his bellboys, Willie runs to the kitchen to get a dustpan and mop. At this very moment, René Poignal, the local police detective and friend of the establishment, strolls down the hall with the remark, "*Qu'est ce que ce passe? Mon Dieu, quel gâchis!*"

"I know it's a mess, René," Jean-Luc says, looking ready to cry. "It's also a crime. I'm glad you're here. This man..." Jean-Luc is beginning to sputter with rage. "He threw the armoire on the ground breaking all my...my..."

Nelson is still standing by the offending wall, arms now crossing his chest, belligerent. His nose is lifted high.

"I can see," says René calmly. "Quite destructive!" He walks warily around the broken glass and broken bellboys, as Willie is trying to sweep the pieces into a neat pile in a corner of the office.

"Careful, Willie," Jean-Luc says anxiously. "There might be a whole one left…" His face betrays doubt.

"I know, sir, I know," Willie is mumbling as he performs his humble task.

"Hello, Jean-Luc," I say shyly, going to the hotelier.

"Ah, Elizabeth. Forgive me, please. For you to arrive in this…this…" and he spreads his arms helplessly.

"I am so sorry for you losing all these…" and I too spread my arms. "I know how precious they are to you."

"Indeed, Madame. I have collected them for years. They were like my little friends…where I came from. Bellboy was my first job." And again, Jean-Luc looks about to cry.

René has taken Nelson from the office, in fact outside the building and is talking to him on the street. I can see him through the front glass doors of Hotel Marcel. Nelson is particularly animated, waving his hands, making faces. René is calm, controlled. In minutes, they separate, René returning into the hotel and coming down the hall to Jean-Luc's *bureau*.

"Are you going to press charges?" he asks Jean-Luc in French.

"*Mais oui!*" is the emphatic answer.

"Are you sure you want to?" René asks in English, giving me an appealing look.

"*Pourquoi pas?*" Jean-Luc says, his tone resolute.

"Sit down," René says to Jean-Luc, who does so, sinking into his chair behind the desk. "You know, it's trouble. And it's expensive! I made Nelson agree to paying you the cost of the armoire and the objects that are broken…"

"You can't put a price on my bellboys." Jean-Luc is adamant.

"I know how important they were to you," I interject, "but René is right. A lawsuit could cost you a fortune."

Jean-Luc is sullen in his chair.

"By the way," René remarks. "Guess who's back in town! My roving *frère* – Giscard!"

"Another welding Exposition?" I inquire. Giscard Poignal's profession is welding metal objects for industrial purposes. His studio/workplace is in Barcelona.

"That's right. They hold one every autumn at The Grand Palais." René turns to Jean-Luc. "Could you put him up again? Here at the hotel?" René looks at Jean-Luc. "Hey, *mon ami*, are you listening?"

Jean-Luc shakes himself out of his funk. "Okay. Okay. He can stay. But I can't get out of my head this whole damn fight over the fact that the *Fusion* dining room is losing money. I can't believe Nelson would go to such lengths...throwing my armoire to the ground, breaking ...everything."

"Well, you were right...telling him the food in his dining room is awful. In fact, it stinks!" I say, at which René smiles, and even Jean-Luc's eyes reflect amusement. "Why don't you ruin that dining room further... that would be a real payback!"

"How? How can I do that?" Jean-Luc says listlessly.

"Could you ever serve special little dinners here?" I pose the question enthusiastically. "Not every night, of course...but you have that brand new Cornu stove in your apartment just across the street, where you could create real duck *à l'orange* or *coq au vin* – then bring it over to the little kitchen here to warm it up..."

"The kitchen here is so small," Jean-Luc says slowly, but I can see he is intrigued.

"That doesn't matter. There is a cooking range – a refrigerator - and even a microwave for warming up sauces and such..." I say hurriedly.

"I suppose it's possible." Jean-Luc's forehead is furrowed in thought.

"Of course it's possible," I say happily. "Why not? You have that magnificent stove just across the street to do the important cooking – and it's only seconds to transport it here...and *voila!*"

"*Quelle idée!*" Jean-Luc is beginning to smile.

"And think of the money!" I say with growing gusto. "You could charge plenty – for such a special, true French *diner* – even pulling important guests from The Majestic clientele to partake..." As I expound, Jean-Luc is on his feet.

"Madame Elizabeth. You are a genius! Yes. Yes. I can do it. You know I first trained as a chef…"

"I know. You are a *chef de cuisine par excellence!* I have eaten your wonderful dishes, Jean-Luc. And besides, it would be such fun." I am elated.

Willie pipes up and approaches René, who is listening quietly, shaking his head. "Is it legal, Monsieur René? Can he open a restaurant?"

"It won't be a restaurant, Willie," Jean-Luc breaks in. "It will be by invitation only. And it will be expensive!"

René is beginning to nod in assent. "I can have the health inspectors check over your apartment kitchen and of course, the little kitchen here, in advance, just to make sure" the policeman says, slowly. I rush over and kiss him on the cheek.

"And of course, I will speak to my lawyer – you know him, Elizabeth…" Jean-Luc says, coming toward me.

"Jacques Ballon?" I ask.

"*Exactement,*" Jean-Luc responds. "He will see I don't break the law."

And it is decided: The Exclusive Hotel Marcel Dining Club. *Un Cercle Privé.*

Eh bien! All is settled.

The first thing I always do, as I arrive in my room on the 5th floor of Hotel Marcel, is to go out on the balcony. There I reconnect with The Eiffel Tower, looming magnificently above – pay my respects – and then view the three apartments across the street where I have seen such drama happen in the past: from dinner parties to murder, from lustful play to dangerous *liaisons.*

It appears to be all quiet on the apartment front. The rooms on the 5th floor of the first two buildings are shuttered. Of course, Jean-Luc owns the apartment in building number two, and he is busy downstairs in his hotel. I wonder where Sylvie LaGrange is – the merry widow in building number one. Is she still in hot pursuit of the good doctor, Guillaume Paxière?

The only sign of life is the face of Henriette, the *femme de ménage* of the Frontenac's domicile nearest to The Eiffel Tower. She appears in the cupola at the top of the building, the third in the row I am inspecting. There she is, still in her bird's nest - Henriette - puffing a *Gauloise* – *comme d'habitude* –and breathing in the air – between puffs.

As I stand there, I can only marvel at the new project for my small hotel. Jean-Luc will be in the business of providing superior dinners to an elite selection of people! I go into my room and reach for a cigarette, then return to the balcony and smoke it in silent communion with Henriette.

Watch out, *Fusion* – and your famous Japanese *chef*, Atari! You're in for some real competition.

La Cuisine Française authentique! By a master *chef*.

CHAPTER 4

Delicious Moments

BRIT PICKS ME up around 5:00, and we are off to his little house in the Marais district to spend the rest of the weekend in private intimacy. It has been more than five months since we have been together. Our need for each other is at its height, and we are eager to be alone.

As the early evening turns into night, I begin to emerge from the haze of love and am able to appreciate the beauty of the canvasses Brit has placed against his bedroom walls and downstairs in the salon.

"You should see the ones I brought over to the gallery on St. Honoré earlier today. They are my best," he insists.

"But these, Brit," I exclaim. "The color is breathtaking – and the architectural ones – there is always the sense of life pulsing behind the pigment and interwoven into the abstractions."

"You're the perfect critic!" he says, coming forward, holding me.

"I can't wait for the show. LUDWIG TURNER (Brit), British/ American abstract painter *extraordinaire!* When is it to take place?"

"It starts Tuesday, November10th. Now, Miss Elizabeth, I'm hungry. Let's eat."

Dinner is late. We walk over to *La Cocotte*, the evening cool and fresh, hand in hand, and sit before their small coal fire in its grate. The *plat* is, of course, the *poulet bonne femme*, braised in cream and *champagne*. It is the specialty of the restaurant. *La Cocotte* is famous for it.

It is a dish for lovers – aromatic, the cream sauce scented with the elegant wine with nothing to disturb the pure taste. A warm *baguette* and a glass or more of *champagne*…ah, well. What more could one desire?

On Monday, I will be staying at Hotel Marcel. Brit needs his space to finish off paintings for the exhibit across the Seine. It promises to be a spectacular show. But we have this night and all day tomorrow with the night that follows to be enchanted with each other.

And that we are. On Sunday, I decide to cook on his little gas stove. I make, of all things, a *chouxfleur gratinée*, the cauliflower florets steamed, then baked in a *béchamel* (white sauce) and topped with *Gruyère*.

I also create a duck *confit*, with *sautéed* potatoes, the dish redolent of the duck fat and absolutely delicious.

Brit is truly impressed. "Now how did we get into the love of food to such a degree?" I ask him.

"I don't know, but it only adds to the grace of life. Keep cooking, sweetheart, it becomes you!"

The grace of life! Of course, it is not only food. First and foremost, it is love, and then of course, the beauty of art. We have the time for love and also, for me, a chance to really explore the works he has created. My Brit is a master. He is becoming known, not only in Paris, but in London as well, where his paintings are shown more and more frequently at Durant, a distinguished art emporium that boasts an excellent and wealthy clientele.

Brit's showing at the Fernand et Fils Gallery on the rue St. Honoré, is not the first exhibition he has had at the esteemed gallery. Surely it will not be his last. The senior Fernand, owner and art enthusiast, loves Brit's vision and, in fact, has purchased three pieces for his home in Neuilly. I am eager for the evening when Brit will be lionized.

Love. Art. *Cuisine d'amour*. And a Paris in which to taste it.

CHAPTER 5

Circy Couture
"A Cut Above"

I COME TO meet Circy Detweiler at Isabella and Jean-Luc Marcel's apartment across the street from his hotel. He invites me – with Brit – for a welcoming cocktail on Monday evening.

Circy Detweiler is a small woman with curly brown hair and a wide mouth. My immediate impression of her outfit is that it resembles a presentation from the *Fusion* dining room at the Majestic Hotel – a mixture of colors and textures and odd combinations: fringed salmon color short boots; a patterned peasant dress from somewhere in the Middle East in orange and red (pepper strips?); an oyster-color wispy scarf. This Circy is a new and up-and-coming designer of clothes? (I'll stick to Isabella's Yves St. Laurent!)

She is obviously an ambitious woman. She seems to fancy herself as very *au courant* and ready to embrace the *nouvelle culture* in France. Of course, it is mostly self-induced pretense. Circy is from Queens, a borough in New York. But she has a street gift of seeing and knowing what moves the frantic little women and girls who long for celebrity.

Circy is sitting on the sofa, scarfing down Jean-Luc's warm cheese puffs, sipping a glass of *Pinot Noir*. On the floor, at the edge of one booted foot, is a large handbag. It is white patent leather, with gold metal attachments.

"Circy's Herbal Essence *Parfums et Colognes,*" she expounds. (Her French pronunciation is horrible!) "These are real perfumes – not some cheap little herbal creams for the skin. No. No. These are perfume – on the level with Chanel #5 and Miss Dior," Circy says proudly. "And of course, we have the spray cologne – but again with the actual attar, the perfumed oil of the real herb! The basil is sensational. If a scent can have a color, the basil perfume smells green."

"I guess the dill would too," Brit remarks, as Jean-Luc gives him a grin.

"Oh yes, of course it does, but less earthy," Circy says.

"The mint, too, pretty green," I say, joining in the fun. Circy ignores this. "I call it 'Sweet Basil,'" she says primly.

"Why not 'Basilisk'?" Brit says.

"What's basilisk?" I ask him, smiling.

"It's a kind of lizard," is his reply.

"What?" Circy is offended.

"It has spellbinding eyes, apparently," Brit finishes.

I realize this American woman is attempting to impress Isabella, our Yves St. Laurent designer, perhaps in order to have the famous couture house showcase her perfume products.

I discover later that this is true, that Circy is determined Yves St. Laurent carry her perfumes, on consignment. She has been pursuing Isabella for several days. Isabella has reached a pinnacle of power in the St. Laurent *atelier*, after only a couple of years. And well she should! A more competent (and charming) young woman could not be found. Jean-Luc is justifiably proud.

I am dubious Isabella is enthusiastic about what Circy is trying to sell, but who knows. Business is business.

"What do you think of 'Madame Cut Above'?" I ask Brit as we leave the Marcels and drive across Paris to his house next to the Place des Vosges in the Marais.

"Who?" he questions, looking at me curiously.

"This Circy person. That's her brand name. 'A Cut Above'."

"Who knew?" Brit says with a laugh. "Well, she's a real 'type'. Very ambitious obviously. I don't honestly think her pursuit of Yves St. Laurent – in terms of displaying and selling her herby scents - will pay off. Sounds crackpot to me – but hell, I'm no connoisseur of a lady's perfumes…"

"Me too," I say, lazily. "'A Cut Above. Circy Couture!'" and we proceed across Paris on our way to his small kitchen to prepare an omelet, drink half a bottle of *Chardonnay* and slip upstairs to his narrow bed near the easel facing the window.

CHAPTER 6

Le Voisinage
(The Neighborhood)

TUESDAY MORNING, BRIT drops me back at Hotel Marcel. As I enter the lobby, I see Giscard Poignal at the front desk talking to Willie. He turns and greets me with warmth. I must say he is as handsome as ever, as he approaches me, kisses my hand, and smiles.

"You're here for another Exposition, I understand," I say.

"Why yes, Elizabeth. It always inspires me to see the artistic work an anvil can produce."

"Maybe you'll get into the art world of welding yourself, one of these days."

"I doubt it," he says, letting go of my hand. "I don't have the imagination."

"I doubt that," I say, thinking of how 'imaginative' he was last year in seducing Bonny Brandeis. But I shan't let my mind go there. With Giscard, his sexuality always seems to…what? Dominate?

I go up to my room to change clothes, then out on the balcony. There is still no action on the other side of the street in my theater of the three apartments. Nobody's home.

I descend in my black coat with its imprints of rosy feathers, strategically placed. Giscard is still talking with Willie and as I pass he calls to me. "How grand you look, Elizabeth," which brings a blush to my cheeks (to match the feathers) and a bounce to my step.

I am on my way to buy a small leather case for Brit. There is no reason, no birthday, nothing other than my feeling for my artist. He is in need of a container for some very special colored pencils and chalks he works with. There is an art store on the next street, avenue Bosquet, where I am sure to find the perfect container.

As I pass *Le Nôtre*, the elegant food emporium in the neighborhood, I see through the window, Henriette peering into the glass case at the prepared *salades, les oeufs mayonnaises*, some browned chicken legs, ham from Parma, cheeses. I decide to accost her and hear of the whereabouts of the Frontenacs, the family in apartment number three.

"Madame," Henriette says cordially, as she turns from the cold case as she hears me speak her name.

"I'm so pleased to see you, Henriette. How are you and how are Monsieur and Madame Frontenac?"

"All is well," she responds in her halting English. "Right now they are with Monsieur Duke and Mrs. Lilith in Chicago. I am – how you say it – I am guard of the apartment while they are away – really *une vacance* for me...a whole month. They just left."

"Oh, I'm sorry I won't see them."

"They will be sorry too. You know, Madame, there is a new little baby girl...Eliza."

"How adorable!"

"Yes, only a few months old. Monsieur Frontenac...so excited. He is *grand-père*...so proud," and she giggles.

"You must be lonely without them."

"*Non. Non.* I have other *femmes de ménage* nearby. We meet at the supermarket or here at *Le Nôtre* or take a *café* at a bistro. We *bavarder...*" Henriette pauses.

"You gossip?" I ask with a smile.

"Yes! We gossip," she answers happily. "You know...the *voisinage...*"

"Neighborhood?"

"Yes. Yes. Neighborhood."

"Do you ever see Madame LaGrange?"

Henriette starts to laugh. "Oh, *mon Dieu, toujours...* with the *docteur...* and then there is the romance of Monsieur Blakely and the little Asian woman who works at The Majestic."

"You know about that?" I am surprised.

"The whole street knows. But Monsieur Blakely should be careful. She is danger."

"Ana Wi? Dangerous?"

"Not to trust," Henriette says, wagging her finger. "She is also *amie de* Japanese *chef* at *Fusion.*"

"You hear this from your friends on the street?"

"Oh, yes," Henriette replies. "They all speak of how... she creeps around...and...she 'busies' herself with men..."

"Oh, *mon Dieu,* I exclaim. This is news.

We embrace as she prepares to purchase a shrimp salad, and I head out the door. Ana Wi! I have only seen her once talking to Willie at the front desk. Such a quiet little one. Who could imagine! It's strange that such an inscrutable person could be so stealthy...but promiscuous?

Dear old Henriette. I remember Elise Frontenac telling me how, one Christmas, early in Henriette's service with them, she and Pierre decided to give their loyal employee a trip home to Alsace to see her family as a holiday treat. Much to the Frontenacs' astonishment, Henriette rushed from the apartment in tears. *"Jamais,"* she cried. *"Jamais."*

When she returned, tear-stained and contrite, she explained she hated the old country, even her family, that she loved Paris, loved running daily to the market (three times a day) to buy the morning *baguette,* at noon the ripest tomatoes, at 5:00 PM the freshest fish for dinner and to *bavarder* with her peers. That was the end of Henriette's homecoming.

As distracted as I am, I find the perfect leather case for Brit that I will deliver to him this evening with all my love. And with all the overflowing good thoughts in my head, I keep thinking of Henriette's words, her gossip, her awareness of all around her. Sometimes it pays to *bavarder!* It certainly pays to listen. So Ana Wi is two-timing our Willie Blakely. Fair warning.

And with of all people, Yoki Atari.

CHAPTER 7

Fusion Confusion

IT IS ABOUT as confused an evening as I have ever spent! No kidding. Our table? Brit, myself, Jean-Luc and Isabella, Ray Guild, editor of Paris *Vogue* magazine, with Sasha Goodman, the well-known *Vogue* photographer, and of course, our hostess: Circy Detweiler.

More than confusion, it is a disaster.

Circy has invited us to dine in the *Fusion* dining room of The Majestic, partly to impress the hotel, but also to convince our party that the food is worth eating. When she had asked us, at Jean-Luc's apartment on Monday night, all of us had expressed a concern about *Fusion's* menu and the fact that much of the *entrées* and *plats* were, well, frankly, quite inedible.

"That's ridiculous," Circy countered. "All I know is that every morning, I order room service from the *Fusion* menu and the most delectable breakfast arrives. I have it every day – a mushroom *omelette*, almost like a *soufflé* with creamy mushrooms on top. Sometimes it has a sprinkle of cheese …it is to die for… so good," she says with a smile. "I know the *chef* can do wonderful things. It's all in what we order."

Reluctantly, the four of us agree. I see a glint in Jean-Luc's eye. Perhaps, being there will send a message to Nelson, that his outrageous performance in Jean-Luc's office, has not curtailed in the least the activities of the proud owner of Hotel Marcel.

So, we find ourselves at a table for seven people on this Wednesday evening in the dining room, *Fusion*, at The Hotel Majestic next door to Jean-Luc's Hotel Marcel. Ray Guild, (pronounced Gild), and photographer, Sasha Goodwin, have been invited by Circy because the prestigious magazine is planning a layout of pictures of her dresses for the fall issue. This is her way of cementing the deal.

Ray has confided in me that he is not happy with the magazine's arrangement with Circy Couture. "The problem is, she's highly successful in the states. The REAL problem for me is, I hate the clothes!"

The large black menu books arrive for our selection. We all chose a variety of *plats*. Over cocktails – mostly *Kir Royals* – a dry martini for Ray - we chatter on about the newest trends in clothes. Circy is wearing a bright yellow dress with a pale green cowl neck, and again, the pinkish suede fringed boots.

When her dinner plate arrives, poached salmon with garish strips of lemon zest and a pool of greenish dill and cucumber sauce, dots of avocado chunks and yellow squash, Ray cannot help but burst out with the remark, "Why Circy. Your outfit matches your plate!"

Our hostess swallows this comment, looking disgruntled, then tastes the food. "It's ice cold," she blurts. "The salmon is supposed to be hot!" this said as she removes the cold piece of fish unceremoniously from her mouth. (Brit and I had the foresight to order *steak/frites*, the only 'normal' dish on the menu.)

"Take this back," Circy says in a loud voice to the waiter, who has rushed to her side. "This is disgusting." She drops her napkin to the floor. Actually, she hurls it there in a fit.

"Do you wish to order something else?" the poor man inquires. "Here, here is the menu." He is proffering the large black book.

"No, no. Take that away. And take this…this cold piece of fish with you. I want nothing more," Circy says haughtily, downing a full glass of *Cabernet Sauvignon* to ease her disgruntlement. "I'm afraid you were right, Jean-Luc. The food…ugh…how's yours, by the way?" she asks, pointing to his dish of shrimp on a sauce of *vichysoisse* with beet chips as accompaniment.

"Cold," is Jean-Luc's answer.

Ray has ordered a second martini. He has not touched his dish of rather portly scallops resting on folds of lasagna pasta sheets with nubs of pancetta. "I'm drinking my dinner as you can see," he says slyly to Circy. "Mine's cold too. And what an odd combination," he continues, looking at his plate with disgust.

"This is outrageous," Circy declares. The waiter, who is standing beside her chair moves uncomfortably from one foot to the other. "I want to see the *chef*," she says, again in a loud voice.

Other diners are watching. I notice the obnoxious couple from Georgia -what were their names – ah yes, Madge and Jerry. I had seen them over the past few visits. They seem to come to Paris as often as I. Tonight they are peering avidly at our table and the commotion going on.

Not to be noticed at the far end of the room, sitting alone, is a man in a gray suit. He is observing the Circy *débâcle* with interest, as he tries to eat several items from the menu, not all at once, of course, but in sequence. Unbeknownst to those in the dining room, this man is Henri Bresson, food critic and writer for *Haut Art Culinaire*, the foremost magazine on the *cuisine* of France, not only covering Paris but with reviews as far flung as Lyon and Marseilles.

Monsieur Bresson has a small notebook at his side, and occasionally, he will scratch some words in it with a Bic pen. Very unobtrusively. But his eye is fixed on the scene unfolding in the center of the dining room.

The *Fusion chef*, Yoki Atari, a small, Japanese gentleman with a thin moustache, wearing his white smock and with his *chef's* toque upon his head, appears at Circy's table. He stands before her, silent, frowning.

"The food I ordered was ice cold! So it was tasteless. Even my guests were unhappy with their food. Everything should be served piping hot. It arrived miserably cold." She looks at the sour face before her. "I am sorry, *chef*, but I don't understand. Your mushroom omelet for my morning breakfast is so outstanding."

Monsieur Atari doesn't speak, but his eyes are furiously red.

There is silence throughout the large room, all diners' attention on this confrontation.

I notice Madge and Jerry whispering together. They have recognized me and send a little, surreptitious wave in my direction, which I do not acknowledge. Madge's dimples and perennial smile are in evidence. And Jerry's pompous body language makes it clear they are very, very rich. I discover later, they are staying in Suite 555 of The Maj. Always contemptuous of the 'dinky little Hotel Marcel,' they look at this moment quite delighted with the embarrassing situation befalling the owner of said Hotel Marcel and – including *moi*.

In any encounter, we have never hit it off, to put it mildly.

"Madame." The *chef* finally spits out furious words. "You make scene. This is unacceptable. You do not like my food. Not necessary to eat in my dining room!" And with a flourish, for a man as small as he, he turns on his heel and marches back to his kitchen.

Madge and Jerry start to clap, as do several of the other diners.

At this moment, who arrives in a flurry but Nelson! He is alarmed by the ruckus in his dining room, furious with Circy Detweiler, and humiliated that Jean-Luc is sitting there at the table.

Circy is on her feet. "Enough of this," she says loudly, throwing a bunch of euros on the table. "Let's go," and it is her moment to march out of the room, the rest of us slowly following behind her.

"Yes indeed," Nelson bellows after us. "I hope *Fusion* and the rest of The Majestic Hotel has seen the last of you." With that, I see him look around wildly. He notices Jean-Luc who is still sitting at the table with an amused look on his face.

"And you, Marcel," Nelson shrieks, shaking his fist. "You are at fault here – with your disparaging remarks and nasty *critiques* of the *chef!*"

"Oh, please Monsieur Nelson. I can't help the way he cooks," Jean-Luc says, his voice off-hand, rising to leave.

Nelson, now furious, shouts, "None of this happens unless you are around. Now go. Get out!" The manager finds himself suddenly self-conscious, embarrassed, and turns swiftly in the direction of the lobby, defeated.

I can't help but grin. "I'm hungry," I whisper in Brit's ear.

"Me too, but not for dinner," he says, kissing the top of my head. As we leave, I notice the man in the gray suit at a table near the exit, his open notebook beside his plate. Just as we pass, I see him slap the cover of the notebook down, with an extremely smug smile. What's that all about, I can't help but wonder, but the thought passes as Brit and I practically run up the street to our haven on the 5th floor of Hotel Marcel.

CHAPTER 8

Whacking Lobsters

I NEVER SAW anyone whack lobster with such gusto as Jean-Luc! He is mad! And the poor crustaceans' shells are being pulverized.

I start to laugh. Jean-Luc looks up from his task in the open kitchen of his apartment. The blue Cornu stove is behind him, and he has just removed three cooked lobsters from a large pot of boiling water, put them on a carving board and has gone at them with a heavy mallet, a long knife, and even a hammer.

Whack! "That one's for Nelson," he exclaims. Whack!

"This is for his long nose!" Whack! "And this for his super inflated ego and superior *attitude!*"

By this time, after this performance, we are all laughing, gathered together on couch, sofa and wing chairs – Brit, Isabella, my dear American friend, Sue de Chevigny, her companion, Franco de Peverelli, and me.

We are here, near 6:00 o'clock, on this Thursday evening, after the *Fusion* fiasco last night, the purpose, an experiment...the first meeting of the *Cercle Privé* of the Hotel Marcel, the dining club Jean-Luc is planning to launch across the street in the hotel salon. It is a gathering to plan, and also to taste Jean-Luc's creation. We are here to choose the date of the first private *diner*, make lists of *invités*, (eight for each dinner), decide menus, and the price of admission.

"We should really have asked Willie Blakely to join us tonight for he will be the general factotum...you know, addressing the logistics of the whole project," Isabella announces with a sigh.

"Yes," responds Jean-Luc. "He will help in the delivery of the food from one side of the street to the other. By the way, did I mention he has a girlfriend? Her name is Ana Wi – an Asian woman. She works at The Majestic as *femme de chambre*." He pauses. "Hey, that's kind of interesting. She might be able to help..."

"Careful, Jean-Luc," Brit interjects. "She's part of The Maj establishment...might not want to lose her job."

Hm. I think of Henriette's remarks about the strange little Asian woman, Ana Wi. I do not mention Henriette's suggestion of Ana's duplicity. It is not the moment.

Through this, Jean-Luc is busily extracting the meat from the lobsters. He is creating a dish he plans to serve at his 'by invitation only' exclusive Hotel Marcel Dining Club, which we are to appraise with the *champagne*, already poured, being enjoyed around the coffee table in the salon.

Jean-Luc wheels forth a small *chef's* station, a movable table with a grill on top. In a large copper *sauté* pan, he places butter, the lobster pieces, heavy cream, and, after stirring, in goes a half-cup of *cognac*. He ignites the dish, and as the flames burn down, serves the '*Homard Jean-Luc*' to us on five plates.

"My God. This is delicious!" Brit exclaims.

"Sublime," breathes Sue.

"*Extraordinaire! 'Homard Jean-Luc*'," Franco bursts out.

And I? I am too busy savoring the succulent dish to say a word.

After a moment, Jean-Luc manages to speak. "Well?"

"This is a must!" exclaims Isabella. She has a large yellow pad at her elbow and proceeds to write down the words '*Homard Jean-Luc*.' "This should be the main course at the first dinner, a specialty. *Cheri*, can you make it for as many as eight people?" she says, turning to her husband.

"But of course," Jean-Luc responds proudly. "The main work can be done right here – the lobster part. I can bring it over, and all the rest will be done right there in the salon, on my *chef's* station, at the end of the long table, for all to see." He raises his glass. "And *champagne!*" Jean-Luc kisses his fingers. "*Fusion* be damned. And Monsieur Nelson too."

This sends us into gales of laughter.

The first dinner is set. Isabella will have invitations created. The date is chosen, Monday, the 2nd of November. It is now to decide WHO to invite...a group of eight that will rile the dining room next door and send Nelson into another paroxysm of rage.

"How did you manage to get such lobsters?" Brit wants to know.

"The lobsters – or *homards* in French - are from your state of Maine... well, in truth, their flavor is unsurpassed. Nothing here can touch their texture and sweetness," Jean-Luc answers.

"How right you are," I say, thinking of the many summers I had spent near Bar Harbor as a young girl and the treat of a lobster roll by the sea. "But, this dinner club," I say. "American lobsters? Isn't the *Cercle Privé* supposed to be '*tout à la francais*'? *Non?*"

"Of course," is Jean-Luc' rejoinder. " '*À la FAÇON francaise!*' ' In the French manner.' We love your lobsters," he says, turning to Brit. "And we also love Iranian caviar and Russian blinis and *choucroute garni*....you know, originally from Germany, then Alsace. This – our *Cercle Privé*, our new dining club, is to present all these – and other dishes of course - in the French fashion."

"Can you get Mane lobsters easily?" Brit asks.

"There is only one place in Paris that I am aware of that flies in Maine lobsters on a daily basis," Jean-Luc continues. "And of course, I went to him. He will be delighted with my next order...the one for Monday, the 2nd of November. I will need at least eight lobsters – perhaps one more for the pot..." Jean-Luc is tapping his chin thoughtfully.

"Good Lord," I say. "Can you imagine the whacking that will take place? Eight – no, nine – crustaceans."

"They will never know what hit 'em," Brit says with a smile.

"And for what a great cause," I say, rising and going to Jean-Luc. "I think you've got a real winner here. The Exclusive Hotel Marcel Dining Club. *Un Cercle Privé*. And, of course, By Invitation Only!"

CHAPTER 9

Mon Appétit!
Jeudi, Oct. 30th

FUSION, THE DINING room in *The Majestic Hotel in the 7th arrondissement, is a total enigma. The ambiance is elegant. The décor, all black and white, is to say the least, chilly. And unfortunately, because the food is presented as an art form, rather than as something to savor with the palate, it often arrives equally chilly!*

It must take the noted chef from Japan, Monsieur Yoki Atari, as well as his sous-chefs, many minutes to create patterns of pepper strips, puddles of sauces, and ribbons of aspic that surround and adorn the cooling duck breast, the tepid capon leg, the wilting shrimp.

It is a travesty. The flavors are there. The spicing is spot-on. But each plat is downright cold by the time it arrives before the diner. Is all this creative time-consuming nonsense necessary? I think not.

It is too late. The frigid damage is done. On the evening I was there, an unpleasant contretemps occurred when, for this very reason, a hostess at a large table confronted the chef, Monsieur Yoki Atari, refused his food, and the party left **Fusion** *in utter disgust.*

Henri Bresson, Food Editor
Haut Art Culinaire

I give **Fusion** *2 stars in a 5 star hotel.*

CHAPTER 10

A New Twist

ON FRIDAY MORNING, on descending for breakfast in the salon, I am met by Willie Blakely at the front desk with the new copy of the fancy magazine, *Haut Art Culinaire.*

On page 34, I find the review by the Food Editor, Henri Bresson, on his experience two nights ago, while dining at *Fusion.* I find his words immensely gratifying. In what an arch manner he expresses his opinions!

In the midst of reading the review, over my *café au lait,* I see Ray Guild stride into the lobby, face bright with morning light. He notices me at my perch on a chair at the table, moves toward me with a loud "*Bonjour,* Madame," and plunks himself down across from me.

"Take a look at this," I say, handing him the open magazine.

"Before you even say 'good morning?'" he says with a grin.

"You'll see why," I reply, breaking into the *croissant* on my plate. I watch his face as he reads, see the growing smile, then hear his chuckle.

"Well, what do you know! Good old Henri Bresson," Ray says, laying down the magazine, closing it, patting it. "*Au fond,* Henri is an actor. He reminds me physically of Clifton Webb. He can appear as a small fellow dressed in gray, seated alone in a dining room, or as a flamboyant fop. It all depends on the establishment."

"What do you mean?" I ask.

"Well, if he wants to sneak into a bistro for a private taste from an unknown *chef*, he will appear innocuous, or on the other hand, he may want to terrify the cook in a fancy restaurant by a very obvious presence – with a bright kerchief in his breast pocket and hat atilt."

I have to laugh. "You would know, Ray. You would know."

"From this" Ray says, patting the magazine on the table again, "you can tell he despises *Fusion*. But he loves the confrontation with Atari and Circy Detweiler. Food and its presentation and ultimately, its savor – these are sacrosanct to him. The miserable *froideur* of his own dinner, well, to see the little *chef* and the rather loud and brassy Circy in conflict over the icy food….well, it must have been a reaffirmation of his own experience."

As I look over at the front check-in desk, I see that Willie Blakely is deep in conversation with the small, Asian woman, dressed in the gray uniform of a housekeeping worker at The Hotel Majestic.

This is Willie's girlfriend that Jean-Luc mentioned (and that Henriette warned me about). She is leaning on the top of the desk, one hand outstretched toward Willie. She has the most gentle smile upon her face. His returning smile is in kind. He catches my eye and beckons me to come over.

I can't resist. "Good morning," I say brightly, as I join the two in the lobby.

"Ah, Madame Elizabeth. May I introduce you to my friend, Ana Wi. She works next door at The Maj."

"Well, how do you do," I say. "I believe I saw you once before, here, talking to Willie." as she turns to me with a little bow, and with the word 'Madame' in a most dulcet voice. I notice her skin is like silk and the small teeth of great whiteness.

"Mamzelle Wi is atelling me that poor Miss Circy is not well. In fact, she is quite sick – with a rash and a dicky stomach – you know, spitting up her breakfast."

Ana Wi is nodding in acquiescence. "Yes," she says quietly. "I am assigned to her room...poor lady. She is so unwell... even her throat closing up. Very alarming."

"Good Lord," I say. "We must get her a doctor."

"Oh, Mister Nelson did that already. A doctor Guillaume Paxière arrived to take care of her," Ana Wi hastens to say.

"Not him again!" I say with vehemence.

"What?" Willie exclaims.

"Oh, it's nothing," I say. "It's just that I know of the good doctor." Silver haired, suave, foxy, no woman is off limits. A few years ago, he was in hot pursuit of me, but was quickly turned away. (Not my type!)

Nothing daunted, soon enough, he was running after my friend, Sue, even though, at the time, she was married to the very attractive Marquis.

Again, rejection, which bothered him not at all. Then, it was poor Sylvie LaGrange, widowed and hungry, and next, Elise Frontenac.

Now apparently it will be Circy's turn. God help her.

"What happened? How did she get so sick?" I ask. At this moment, curious, Ray joins us at Willie's desk.

"Who's sick?" Ray chimes in.

"Miss Detweiler. The doctor thinks it is what she ate. It was yesterday, right after her breakfast. She turned almost blue and ran to the bathroom and I could hear her – retching – poor lady." Ana Wi is wringing her hands.

"What was it she ate that morning," Willie asks.

"It's always the same. A mushroom *omelette*," was Ana's response.

Well, what do you know, I thought. You don't suppose that Yoko Atari just happened to use a poisoned mushroom in his *omelette*? These are not hard to find, and I understand they come in various forms – the Death Cap, the Destroying Angel, Russula, known as the 'sickener' with a peppery taste. The *chef* was surely angry enough after the humiliating scene last Wednesday night!

"Did the doctor say anything about what might have poisoned her?" Ray questions.

"Well, he did seem suspicious of the *omelette*... you know, the mushrooms. The plate was still there, half eaten. But I explained to him," Ana goes on, "Miss Detweiler has a mushroom *omelette* every morning, and he replied 'maybe this time, the *chef* picked mushrooms from the wrong patch.'"

"Could be," I say knowingly.

"You don't think..." Willie is looking at me. He has heard all about our *Fusion* evening ending in disarray.

"It's possible, Willie. Atari was humiliated by her and when I say furious, I mean it!"

And Ana chimes in, "I must say Dr. Paxière was mighty curious. He said 'I've seen mushroom poisoning before, and this seems to be a classic case.'"

"A poisoner in our midst?" Ray says, with a kind of relish.

It seems incongruous, but Yoki Atari, Japanese *chef*, known for diva-like passions in his kitchen, might well be capable of such a vengeful act. If he did the dirty deed, he surely acted quickly!

And Ana Wi. His consort?

The plot gets thicker.

CHAPTER 11

Circy's Predicament

IT IS THE weekend. On Saturday morning, I return to Hotel Marcel after a night with Brit in his Marais house. He joins me for breakfast in the salon before driving over to rue St. Honoré across the Seine to the Fernand et Fils Gallery. He is busily supervising the mounting of his show, which will take place there in a matter of days.

In the hotel lobby, Willie is placing a large vase of flowers on a pedestal. They are put there daily – fresh and fragrant, part of the tradition of this small hotel that makes its charm unique. I ask my cockney friend if he has heard anything from the hotel next door about Circy Detweiler's ailment.

"She be better," he says. "In fact, except for one whole day and one whole night where she couldna keep anything down, but now, she is practically as good as new." He starts to chuckle.

"What's so amusing?" I ask.

"Well, this doctor fella. He practically never leaves her side…giving her little potions he concocts, and she…"

"Yes?" I am all ears.

"She laps it up. Ana says she can't keep her hands off him. Ah, I shouldna say such things."

"It's okay, if it's true," I say knowing full well that Guillaume Paxière is in his element and up to old tricks.

Circy seems to be in her element too – whatever that is – entranced with the typical Paris roué. Oh yes. They exist. Actually, they are one of Paris' ultimate charms.

But *prenez-garde*. Don't fall in love!

Over *café au lait* and *croissants* and wedges of *Gruyère*, Brit and I linger lovingly, saying little but occasionally our hands touch. Giscard Poignal appears from the hall behind the front desk, having descended from his third floor room (Jean-Luc lets him stay for free). He notices the two of us.

"May I join you?" he asks.

I notice Brit wince. Now how can he be threatened? Because Giscard emanates such manly testosterone? Really Brit. I give him a small kick under the table.

As Giscard partakes of a coffee (black) and a portion of *baguette*, I mention how excited I am about Brit's coming show at Fernand et Fils. Our new companion looks up, startled and truly interested, and he and Brit – ignoring me – get into an in depth discussion of modern art. Giscard certainly has his charms, other than the obvious physical attributes. My Brit is now animated and eagerly talking with Giscard, describing some of the difficulties in mounting the show.

"Two small rooms – although one is large enough for the bigger canvasses. I don't know how I can hang them all…"

"Perhaps I can help," Giscard interjects. "I'm pretty good at this stuff. Besides, I'd really love to see your work."

Suddenly, the two are big buddies and Brit invites Giscard to join him. "Right now?" I ask.

"Why not?" is Brit's response. "No time like the present."

There is no room for Giscard in the Peugeot. The rear is stuffed with paintings. "I'll catch a cab," he says, and in due course, I find the three of us in the gallery on rue St. Honoré. Giscard is a blessing and any animus (or jealousy) that Brit has felt is gone for the moment because Giscard suggests some brilliant, innovative ways to display Brit's works of art.

Brit is so pleased, so filled with fresh ideas, he invites Giscard to join us for a late lunch, (Brit's treat!) which Giscard accepts with alacrity. We decide on the dining room of the Crillon Hotel, the gorgeous building (once a Prince's home palace) on the Place de la Concorde.

Over superb *sole meunière*, with brown butter and lemon, and a crackling *Sauvignon Blanc*, we converse, Giscard his compulsively flirtatious self (with me), and Brit growing more sullen by the minute.

No problem, I think. I smile to myself. Wait until I get him home, back to the Marais, and his sweet little house which provides an enclosed world of love and privacy. I have tonight and all day tomorrow to convince my lover that he's the only one. What fun!

CHAPTER 12

'Homard Jean-Luc'

ISABELLA HAS PLACED small, white votive candles down the center of the long table in the salon of Hotel Marcel. Between them, she has put low bunches of white *fleur de lis.* The light in the fringed lamps hanging above the table, she has lowered, as she has kept the music from the intercom, soft. The choice of song, on the machine back in Jean-Luc's office, piped through to the salon, a rendition by an American pianist/vocalist is – what else – "There's a Small Hotel."

The stage is set, this Monday evening November 2nd, in Paris – the first meeting of The Hotel Marcel Dining Club, By Invitation Only.

Maria, one of the house employees is at the front desk, as Jean-Luc closes the double doors between the lobby and the salon. The dining table and its occupants will be enclosed in privacy. The soft music plays. The votive candles and hanging lamps shed their gentle light.

The guests on this first evening – eight of us in all – are Circy Detweiler, eager to test the *chef*, Jean-Luc himself. She is accompanied by her new companion, Dr. Guillaume Paxière. Ray Guild, who plans a special piece about this *Cercle Privé Diner* to appear in French *Vogue*, is at table, as is Sasha Goodwin, who is quietly snapping pictures for *Vogue*. There are La Marquise Sue de Chevigny and Franco de Peverelli, who will embellish the article by their presence, and Brit and myself. We are ready to partake of 'Homard Jean-Luc', which he will *flambé et garni* at his moveable *chef's* station at the front of the room near the closed double doors.

Brigitte is manning the kitchen. Isabella is in position in the salon, pouring the *champagne* in flutes for each of us, with Willie Blakely placing the baskets of warm *baguettes* strategically on the table. He also puts before us, the first course, an *oeuf en gelée*, with a pungent slice of *foie gras* embedded in the glistening aspic.

We are sitting there, barely talking, eagerly awaiting the moment to begin. Jean-Luc, standing at the end of the table, near the doors, welcomes us with a raised glass.

"Mesdames. Messieurs. This first *diner* of The Hotel Marcel Dining Club – is about to commence. I hope you will enjoy what I present to you this evening."

We are about to taste the delightful *entrée* before each one of us, when there is a tap on the partitioning door. Jean-Luc is discomfited. "I told Maria, no one…" There is another tap, slightly louder.

Jean-Luc sets down his glass and opens the door a crack. I see his face filled with surprise, mouth open.

"Monsieur Bresson?"

"*Oui. C'est moi.*"

"Sir, may I ask…?"

"I heard of this special dining experience…"

"Where?"

"At The Majestic, of course. I believe Mademoiselle Detweiler was speaking of it. Apparently her chamber maid told her about it."

By this time, Henri Bresson is in the room. Jean-Luc nods at Willie, who is beaming with Bresson's reference to his new love. Willie pulls up an extra chair at the very head of the table near the kitchen for Henri Bresson. The eight of us are arranged across from each other on either side of the long table. Monsieur Bresson walks regally down to the end to place himself in the catbird seat.

"*Merci*, Monsieur Marcel," he says, as he accept a glass of *champagne* from Isabella, and an *oeuf en gelée* from Willie.

Nobody has said a word.

"Please…"Jean-Luc says to the assembled. "Please, shall we commence?"

And boy. Do we!

As we break into the aspic, the soft egg, I can't help but notice, sitting across from me, the behavior of the good doctor and Circy Detweiler. I had heard from Jean-Luc how eager the American clothes designer was to attend an exclusive dinner party *chez* Hotel Marcel. "On the phone, she was positively dripping with *flatterie!*" Jean-Luc had declared.

Now here she is, thrilled with the exclusivity of it all. And yet, it's amazing to watch how flirtatious she is with Dr. Guillaume Paxière! "Your creations?" he is saying to Circy. She is sitting directly next to him, blushing and flustered by his very presence. "Yes, indeed," she says to him. "My *couture*. Circy Couture. They express my…spirit." Oh, how she bats her eyelashes at him! He, in turn, regards his latest prey from under lowered lids, the sexual gleam obvious.

Henri Bresson is tasting his *oeuf en gelée* oh so delicately. He has no notebook, nor Bic pen next to his plate. However, the expression on his face is inscrutable and does not reveal his assessment of the dish before him, in any manner whatsoever.

We all look at his impassive face and watch for a glimpse of approval. Nothing.

Plates cleared away by Willie and Isabella, Jean-Luc appears with his *chef's* station at the front of the room. His large copper *sauté* pan is at the ready on the heating grill, the mounded lobster pieces on a platter next to it. With a grand gesture, Jean-Luc places the sweet butter into the pan, and as it begins to sizzle, in go the lobster morsels, a pitcher of heavy cream, sprinkle of salt and pepper, and finally a large wine glass of fine *cognac* that our *chef* proceeds to ignite with a flourish.

There are 'oohs' from the eight of us. Henri Bresson is silently watching.

The *'Homard Jean-Luc'*, now crowned with a sprinkle of finely chopped parsley, is parceled out on nine plates and passed to us by Willie and Isabella, who then bring in, for each of us, an individual goblet filled with upright, French twice-fried potatoes.

Dead silence, save for the clinking of forks. (No knives needed).

Again, surreptitious glances are aimed at Henri Bresson.

There is no sign of his reaction to the sumptuous food, as more chilled *champagne* is poured all around.

Suddenly, Franco de Peverelli announces, "This is the most *delicioso homard* I have ever tasted. And Jean-Luc, you make me want to be a *chef!*"

This pleases our host/hotelier mightily. He still stands beside his station, observing the nine of us, savoring the exquisite dish. Of course, his greatest attention is on Henri Bresson.

"Franco, You are a fine *chef* too," Sue chimes in, her loyalty showing. "Say, we should write a cookbook, featuring the wines we are producing at *Le Couvent*. Perhaps Jean-Luc will help us."

"*Le Couvent?*" It is Henri Bresson who speaks.

"Yes," says Sue. It is the name of my *château* in Montoire. The place was originally a convent. We kept the name, but of course it is physically greatly renovated."

"How interesting," Henri responds, wiping his mouth with the linen napkin.

A salad of light greens in a lemon *vinaigrette*, accompanied by wedges of ripe *Brie*, replaces the empty lobster plates.

"Perhaps you will visit us," Franco is saying. "You could taste the wine I am pressing from the Italian seedlings I brought from Tuscany. Some of the results are quite fine."

"Even more interesting," says Henri. "I love a good wine. The newer ones are hard to find...too raw of taste."

Dessert has arrived, glass dishes of *mousseline au chocolat* with a delectable *crème fraiche* atop each, flavored with *framboise*, the raspberry liqueur. This is followed by tiny cups of *espresso* and a tray with an assortment of after dinner cordials.

Again, a silence descends. People sit back, replete. Cigarettes are lighted, a cigar for Henri Bresson from his breast pocket.

It is Ray Guild who brings up the loaded question, the opinion of Henri Bresson on this *Cercle Privé*, The Hotel Marcel Dining Club, By Invitation Only.

"Just what do you think, sir?" Ray asks boldly of the critic.

"About what?" Henri responds with his own question.

Ray, unabashed, asks again. "Just how do you find the dinner at The Hotel Marcel Dining Club? Was it to your liking?"

Henri Bresson is enjoying all this immensely, his moment in the sun, the suspense he is creating for all of us are waiting breathlessly.

He sits back, puffing slowly, cigar smoke aimed at the ceiling. He pauses dramatically. Then, with a sidelong glance at Jean-Luc, he says, "I have only one word."

Then he pauses as we all bend forward.

"Yes, yes," Jean-Luc says, rapidly.

"One word, Monsieur Marcel. *Superbe!*"

With a sigh, Jean-Luc makes a little bow. His project for a dining club of special dishes for special guests has met with a very important seal of approval. Henri Bresson! Jean-Luc now plans to proceed with ardor – every other week – a Monday - or even perhaps weekly - for which people could plan and reserve.

Henri Bresson is rising which breaks Jean-Luc's train of thought. As he reaches Jean-Luc's side, he stands there, quietly. Then, "You have something quite unique, here, sir. The dinner was exquisitely balanced, the presentation charming, but the most important thing, each *plat*, from *entrée* to *dessert*, was delicious. *Mes compliments*, Monsieur.

"*Merci*, Monsieur. I am honored you were here."

"You will see my column in the next days," Henri says, turning to us, still at table, and with a wave of *adieu* leaves through the double doors.

Isabella rushes to her husband. "We are in business, *cheri*! With Henri Bresson's blessing, The Hotel Marcel Dining Club...""By Invitation Only," Jean-Luc chimes in, "will be the rage of *tout Paris!*" Isabella finishes.

CHAPTER 13

Mon Appétit!
Mardi, Nov. 3rd

IT IS WITH delight I bring to the attention of you, my dear readers, a new and quite extraordinary culinary experience I enjoyed only last night.

At a small hotel in the 7th arrondissement, there has been established an exclusive Cercle Privé, The Hotel Marcel Dining Club, By Invitation Only. The owner of the hotel, Jean-Luc Marcel, is also a fine chef, distinguished by impeccable technique, and creator of truly elegant plats. My 'Homard Jean-Luc' sautéed in butter and cream with a hint of cognac was as delectable as any I have ever tasted. And the repast did not stop there.

I would suggest to any of you who are truly discriminating, a visit chez Hotel Marcel would be well advised, to enjoy an exceptional dining event.

Henri Bresson Food Editor
Haut Art Culinaire

I give **The Hotel Marcel Dining Club** *5 stars.*
Tel: 01- 42 88 84 33

The review of the honorable Henri Bresson not only causes a delighted response in Jean-Luc and Isabella, but Brit and I are thrilled for them. And it appeared so quickly.

The prospect of a separate line of business that will bring kudos for the cooking, but a degree of fame to the hotel "is worth its weight in gold," Jean-Luc declares. "Henri Bresson is famous. He has his own television show."

"Maybe he will mention us," Isabella declares hastily.

"He also is known to write a preface for a new cookbook," says Jean-Luc.

"We should tell Franco and Sue that," I say. "They are busily preparing a cookbook…experimenting with his wines. The recipes will be specifically for cooking with *vin*, the very ones from the vineyard at *Le Couvent*. Perhaps Henri might write a forward…"

Jean-Luc is deep in thought. "Henri's review is *étonnement*. Amazing! And don't forget the money! Each place at table costs 200 euros – which when you consider the quality of the food, the time involved in its preparation, not to mention the *champagnes et vins*, is a steal."

This conversation had taken place at the hotel earlier today, after reading the excellent review from Monsieur Bresson.

"I believe Jean-Luc may raise his rates as time goes by," I mention to Brit, as we walk under the arcade of La Place des Vosges near his house. We had driven over to the Marais to relax in his house, and also for him to complete the final touch on a painting for the show.

"I can hardly blame him," Brit reponds. He pauses. "Do you realize, my show is a week from today!" he says nervously.

"Everything will be ready," I reassure him.

Later, as he finishes his work, "I'm starved," he suddenly exclaims, throwing down his brush. "Let's eat."

The little walk only increases our appetite. We stop at a small sidewalk bistro (we go inside – the air is chill) and order *soupe à l'oignon* and Parma ham on a long buttered *baguette*, which we split.

"Sometimes the simplest is the best," he says, eating with enthusiasm. "The French have a way, no doubt. The most elegant, refined dinner and the plainest ham sandwich and good old onion soup…from A to Z… they can do it all."

"Mmm. Mmm," I mumble through bites. "You can say that again.

CHAPTER 14

Gossip

SUE AND I decide we need to do some major shopping and equally major *bavardinage* (gossiping). We choose, not *Caviar Kaspia*, as is our wont, but a restaurant near La Place de la République.

"There are some neat shops in the area," Sue tells me. "A Dior outlet (cheap), a great leather shop with unusual belts and wallets, gloves, frames for pictures, also a store with cashmere goods – shawls, sweaters, even dresses."

I meet her, this Wednesday morning at *Le Chêne*, named for the live oak tree that grows right through the middle of the place. Our table is on the second floor, with windows looking over La Place de la République and the bronze statue of Marianne, the Goddess of Liberty, at its center.

Over a sparkling salad of ripe pear, endive, *Roquefort* cheese crumbles, and toasted walnuts, we fall into a round of gossipy reports on one and all we'd been exposed to. By the way, the salad is a perfect choice to whet the appetite for new, bright-tasting purchases. It is so sharp and sweet in its lemon *vinaigrette*.

"I read the Henri Bresson review of Jean-Luc's new venture this morning. I must say it was a rave! He must be very pleased," Sue says, taking a long sip of her *Sauvignon Blanc*.

"Of course, he's delighted," I concur. "The evening was such a huge success, and the critic's review so positive, Jean-Luc is planning to have another dinner in a week's time."

"So soon?" Sue says. "I'm surprised."

"Well, he was so thrilled with what Henri Bresson wrote, he decided to take advantage of the publicity, I guess, and have an immediate repeat. Nobody expected Henri Bresson last Monday. He was not invited, but it was a *coup* for Jean-Luc. And the dinner was exceptional. Jean-Luc outdid himself."

"And outdid the *Fusion chef*, for sure! What's his name, 'Errato?'"

"No," I say, laughing. "Atari. Yoki Atari." I pause. "Hey, you know… I've mentioned to you before, the name Henriette, haven't I?"

"Sure, the Frontenacs' *femme de ménage*. Why?"

"Well, I ran into her and she told me – oh, first, that Duke and Lilith are parents of a little girl – Pierre and Elise are in Chicago visiting them…"

"How nice," Sue says, "and a new little granddaughter. I bet she's beautiful. After all, Lilith is lovely, and Duke? Well, he is not bad. Not bad at all. What an interesting combination…Arabic and African-American."

"It certainly is. I'm sure Pierre, particularly, is thrilled. Elise too. They never had any kids of their own." I take a slice of pear. "Anyway, the momentous thing Henriette told me was that Ana Wi…"

"Who?"

"She's a chamber maid next door at The Majestic and also Willie Blakely's girlfriend."

"Willie, Jean-Luc's manager?"

"Yes. He used to be a waiter over at The Maj. The big news is that Ana is apparently *chef* Yoki Atari's girl as well. According to Henriette, and the other *femmes de ménage* on the street, Ana is quite the *coquette*."

"No!"

"Yes! But the real problem is, Yoki is out to ruin Jean-Luc. He is so jealous and so miffed at Jean-Luc's new dining club. The *Fusion* dining room is going down the tubes."

"You don't suppose he's dangerous, do you?"

"Well yes," I say. "I think he could be. I believe he tried to poison Circy Detweiler for dissing his cookery."

Sue starts to laugh. "If this were not so serious, it could be a colossal joke!"

"*Le dessert, mesdames?*" the waiter asks us, proffering the menu. "*Les fraises des bois?*"

We both nod, order espressos with the tiny fragrant strawberries, and our discussion turns to Giscard Poignal.

"He's sure good looking," Sue starts. "Enticing."

"A true 'bad boy'," I say with a laugh. "But he's unexpected. He made such a difference for Brit – who is not too keen on René Poignal's younger brother…"

"That's because Brit thinks Giscard finds you pretty cute."

"Oh, stop, Sue."

"Well, it's true," she says lapping up some strawberries in *crème fraiche.*

"I think the two men are getting along better. Giscard came over to the gallery on Saturday to look at the place and made some terrific suggestions to maximize the way the pictures are shown. Giscard – at a friend's workshop - is going to make some metal strips to replace some of the beveled frames. Makes it more modern, very much in keeping with Brit's vision."

"Interesting," Sue says.

"I thought so. And frankly, Brit was impressed."

"I can't wait for the show. By the way, I told you Franco and I are doing a cookbook. Cooking just with wines. Wines created at our little *Le Couvent* winery."

"I think it's brilliant," I say.

"He has a superb dish –*Coq au Riesling* – of course, it's made with our own white wine – not the real German vintage– but it really is delish."

"I can't wait to try it."

"Oh, you will, sweetheart. You will."

With a final reference to Circy Detweiler and her rather hideous logo – a large CD intertwined in red letters – and her even more hideous 'herbal' – basil, cinnamon, thyme, mint - perfumes – rejected by Yves St. Laurent – we ask for *l'addition* and we're off to find some major bargains on our major shopping spree after a major gossip-fest.

CHAPTER 15

A Warning

IT IS LITERALLY two days after Henri Bresson's review of the lobster dinner at Hotel Marcel appears that Jean-Luc receives a disturbing message from the critic himself.

Jean-Luc tells me this, as I pass the front desk where he is sorting mail He also remarks that since the *'Homard Jean-Luc'* evening, the phone has been ringing constantly – "people inquiring about The Hotel Marcel Dining Club – eager to make reservations – even when they hear the price. Most of them don't seem to care what will be on the menu. They just want the…?"

"Exclusivity?" I question.

"Yes. *Exactement!*"

"You must be elated," I say. "What do you have planned for the next dinner – a *boeuf bourguignon* perhaps?"

"I haven't decided yet – perhaps a rack of lamb – but it will be soon. I am more concerned – *pour le moment* - about my appointment with

51

Henri Bresson. He is coming by in a short while…don't know what he has to tell me that is so serious."

"He certainly loved your lobster…*excusez-moi…l'homard*, " I say with a smile.

"I wonder what he wants," Jean-Luc says reflectively, pausing in his paper shuffling.

"Me too," I say.

"You will be the first to know, Madame Elizabeth. I promise."

I continue on into the salon this Thursday morning, where Brigitte has already placed my cup and pot of *café* with a pitcher of warm milk on the table. There is the usual basket of *croissant/baguette* awaiting, which I eagerly attack, smoothing the butter on the crusty bread, and waking up with the hot coffee. I read the International New York Times (formerly the International Herald Tribune), and enjoy the leisurely beginning to the day.

I am in the midst of the op-ed page, when I see Henri Bresson stride into the lobby, his figure purposeful, enwrapped in a dark, fitted overcoat. Jean-Luc comes around from behind the desk, to greet his guest and with a nod to Brigitte to take up duties where he has left off, he leads Monsieur Bresson down the narrow hall to his office. I hear the door shutting behind the two men.

I remain in the lounge area next to the salon dining area. I am too curious to move. I sit on the sofa and make a list of small presents I intend to buy for family and friends at home. I always bring a little something from my favorite city, usually edibles like *macarons* and *chocolats* – but still, a list has to be made so I don't forget anyone.

Of course, it is only an excuse to tarry - and wait for Monsieur Marcel to tell me what Bresson is so worried about. Circy? Atari? *Fusion?* Or is his mission about The Hotel Marcel Dining Club, By Invitation Only?

The interview between the two men does not last long. I see them walk from the back of the hotel, shake hands at the lobby door, and Henri Bresson takes his leave.

Jean-Luc stands still for a moment. His brow is furrowed, and as he turns, he sees me sitting on the lounge sofa, my face upturned and curious. He walks over to me slowly and sits down next to me. I say nothing.

"Well, I'll be damned," he finally remarks.

"What is it?"

"What an odd fellow. Oh, he is nice enough. And I surely appreciate his review— but he's trying to warn me... I am not sure exactly about what."

"You're confusing me," I say.

"Apparently, Atari – you know, the *chef* at *Fusion*, well, somehow he found Henri's home address, appeared at his front door two days ago in the afternoon, 'when I take my pre-prandial nap,' as Henri put it. Atari tried to bribe him to write a special column about the little Japanese's wonderful cooking! Can you imagine such gall?" Jean-Luc makes a face over the last words.

"You're kidding!"

"No. I'm not. Wonderful cooking! Hah! More like a mixed bag of concoctions on an ice-cold plate – maybe pretty to look at, but impossible to eat."

"I'm not sure the mixed bag is that pretty, you know."

"You're right of course. It is all so contrived and such strange combinations – quenelle-shaped steak tartare separated by wobbles of eggplant purée...ugh. Of course, Henri was outraged at the very idea... the very thought that he was bribable."

"How did he leave it?" I ask.

"*Évidement*, Atari got very angry – so did Henri of course, and for a very proper fellow like Henri, an unusual shouting match between the two commenced."

"So Henri lost his cool," I say with a chuckle.

"*Oui*, it is hard to believe. Atari left, furious. But most alarming, his last words were about me."

"What do you mean? About you?"

"I guess the *chef* still thinks I am bad-mouthing his food..."

"Well, we are all doing that," I say, laughing.

"But it was the column Henri wrote about my Dining Club that really ticked Atari off – is that how you say it in English – *en colère?*"

I nod. "Ticked off is right."

"Ticked off Atari to the point of apoplexy. Henri Bresson warned me."

"Warned you of what? Not another arson attempt, like Hamad al-Boudi!"

"No. Not that. But he thinks Atari is dangerous."

I am taken aback. It now seems more than possible that Atari indeed tried to poison Circy! Apparently, for his culinary reputation, the craft that is his life, he is willing to resort to lethal methods!

Is Jean-Luc in real peril?

CHAPTER 16

Au Pied De Cochon
(Pig's Foot)

AU PIED DE *Cochon,* the revered restaurant – which prides itself on never closing its doors – even in the worst of times – is located in the Les Halles section of Paris. I decide to take Jean-Luc there for lunch. It is such a landmark, and my hotelier-friend seems so deeply worried by the looming threat of Yoki Atari!

I think Jean-Luc is in need of 'a fix'. *Au Pied de Cochon* might raise his spirits. He agrees to join me for a late *déjeuner* this Thursday afternoon.

"Just what is that Japanese *chef* capable of pulling?" he says gloomily, as we are handed large menus at the table in the famous restaurant.

"Who knows?" I say.

"I'm certainly never going to eat a morsel of his food again."

"Nor am I," I agree.

"I'm positive now he poisoned Circy with mushrooms. He should be in jail. René even thinks so, but it's impossible to prove."

"I guess it is," I say ruefully.

"Circy is convinced of Atari's foul play, according to Willie."

"Really? She believes it?"

"She will never dine at *Fusion* again, nor order a breakfast mushroom omelette, *bien sûr.*"

"I should think not!" I ask Jean-Luc if Circy mentioned to Ana Wi her assessment of The Hotel Marcel Dining Club experience. "Did our designer friend say anything?"

"Oh, yes," he responds, brightening considerably. "Ana Wi says Circy was ecstatic – partly, of course, she was with her new lover, the doctor. Apparently, after the *mousseline au chocolat*, they made straight for her suite where he spent the night."

"Busily engaged," I say with a snort. Jean-Luc laughs.

"Doesn't surprise me," I say, rolling my eyes. "But did Circy mention the food you presented?"

"Indeed she did! Circy told Ana Wi that she had never tasted lobster like that…thought it – in her words, 'absolutely fabulous'." Jean-Luc chuckles.

I decide this is a moment in which to express to Jean-Luc my concern about Ana Wi. "You know, Jean-Luc, I heard – on the street –"

He laughs. "On the street?"

"Well, from Henriette – you know…"

"The Frontenacs' Henriette?"

I nod. "She told me that Ana Wi…that she's something of a *coquette* – that she's also Atari's girlfriend."

"What?" Jean-Luc is nonplussed. "Ah…poor Willie."

"Jean-Luc, she is not to be trusted."

"Willie would be devastated," he continues, concerned for his friend and manager.

At least I was able to warn Jean-Luc of Ana Wi's duplicity. "What do you plan to serve at the next grand *diner*?" I ask, in order to change the subject.

"*Eh bien,* thinking about it here in *Au Pied de Cochon*, I think maybe a true Alsatian *choucroute garni* will be the *specialité du jour.*"

"Really?" I am a little surprised.

"Of course, the *chef* here does it superbly – classically well – but I can top even him. You know, I am from Alsace," he says proudly. "I know how *choucroute garni* is done!"

"You're sure?" I say with a grin. "Are you going to order it for lunch?" I say, looking at the menu.

"No," he says firmly. "I am having *Pied de Cochon*. Elizabeth, you must try it."

"Really?" I am dubious.

"It's brilliant here – with the *accompagnements*. The things that come with the *Pied de Cochon*. *Sauce diable. Moutard. Cornichons.* And of course, *frites!*"

"Sounds marvelous."

"You know what, Elizabeth, what's best of all with it?"

"What?"

"Ice-cold beer," Jean-Luc says with a big grin.

Jean-Luc's mood of concern is lifted and the shine of confidence is restored, as I see him dig into the bread-crumbed, grilled pig's foot with the succulent, fatty meat of the porker. He dips the skewered morsels into the *sauce diable*, crunches on the *cornichon* pickles, and with sighs of delight, takes long, slow drafts of the beer.

I guess my mission is accomplished! Jean-Luc is his usual ebullient self. He is restored! And all because of a fatty pigs foot, grilled to perfection, with its tasty *acompagnements*, some French fried potatoes, and an icy glass of Alsatian beer

CHAPTER 17

Yoki Atari

JUST WHO IS Yoki Atari? I have heard enough of his 'fame' as a master *chef*, and I have seen his flaws, but who is he really?

A small man, revered as a *chef extraordinaire* – at least in the eyes of his peers – Yoki Atari has an outsized ego that colors everything and everyone he touches. Actually, he is accomplished in matters *cuisinière*, in that his technique for chopping, his delicacy in carving vegetables, his reduction of sauces to their essence, all these are performed with excellence.

We are all aware of his skills.

However, he has distanced himself from the actual consuming of food – from the need for the dish to be appetizingly hot and aromatic when it is presented to the diner. Yoki Atari's supreme focus is on 'presentation', on creating beautiful artwork on a white platter (that could be framed, from the look of it!). Somehow the loss of taste and savor never occurs to him, as time elapses as he puts together his culinary masterpieces.

(We have all been truly disgusted with the chilliness of his expensive repasts.)

He has trained his *sous-chefs* to do the same. Hence, the dining room at *Fusion* has lost luster and customers because who wants a cold dinner, no matter how artfully it is presented.

Because of the loss of trade, evidently, Yoki Atari's ego is dented. In fact, it is quite smashed as he realizes the lack of customers and approbation for his culinary gifts. In reality, he is furious, growing angrier every passing day and ascribing blame, not only to Henri Bresson, but to Jean-Luc Marcel as well, the latter being so obviously disapproving of Atari's creations. And Circy Detweiler! Well, he is only sorry the mushrooms in her morning *omelette* failed to really harm her, truly do her in.

When The Hotel Marcel Dining Club comes into being and Henri Bresson writes a rave review, Yoki Atari loses it, according to the gossip from next door, transmitted by Ana Wi to Willie Blakely. Apparently, it is then he decides drastic measures must be taken.

First, Yoki attempts to bribe the food critic, to have him write a decent article about Atari's skills and delicious creations. This is rejected out of hand, by Henri Bresson, much to the *chef's* humiliation and ultimate fury. In fact, the *chef* attacks the critic verbally in Bresson's own home.

Second, he decides to disrupt Jean-Luc's new enterprise. Yoki has heard of the exquisite lobster dinner, not only from Bresson's review, but the buzz about it has filled the dining room at The Majestic – from the waiters to the few customers – even from the American couple who still continue to eat at *Fusion* – even they – Madge and Jerry something! They are determined to attend the next dinner at the Hotel Marcel, to join the *Cercle Privé*. 'It's by invitation only,' a waiter tells Yoki in the kitchen one evening. He has heard the remark in passing their table. Nothing daunted, Jerry and Madge are already on a cell phone to Jean-Luc.

This stops the *chef* cold (as cold as one of his food creations!) It is the moment. Yoki Atari makes up his mind that something must be done, and right now!

His mind begins to hatch a plan, (in Japanese, of course). His mental process goes something like the following.

I am a knife expert. No. Too obvious.

I know poisoning. It is an art, but perhaps, again, too obvious because of the mushroom omelette, its failure and the attention it caused. That damned doctor!

I must be careful.

Aha! I will make that bloody *Monsieur Marcel's food noxious. I can put dirt into his dishes – or insects, creepy crawlies – or hair.*

Because Marcel must bring his main dishes from across the street – or so my little Ana Wi has told me – because they leave his main oven to go to the small hotel kitchenette – this is the perfect time to contaminate. At the time of the crossing! It will take pinpoint planning. I believe – according to Ana, that his manager Willie something – the poor fool is in love with my Ana – Ha! He used to be a waiter in my Fusion dining room, disloyal fellow – he will be the one to carry the hot dishes on the journey from one kitchen to the other. I must find out exactly when the second dinner will be taking place and what the plat for the evening will be. Ana will let me know, when we are in bed together, in plenty of time.

I will devise a very special addition to the flavor of the dish – perhaps a potent herb that ruins the whole – or I really like the idea of creepy crawlies! That should kill off the evening royally, and the reputation of the pretend chef, Jean-Luc Marcel! I can't wait to read Henri Bresson's review of that particular Hotel Marcel Dining Club – By Invitation Only – dinner party.

Yes indeed! Yoki Atari has a plan!

CHAPTER 18

The Perfect Wine

IT'S FRIDAY, AND the weekend is ahead before the second of The Hotel Marcel Dining Club extravaganza is to take place. Monday night! November 9th, the evening before Brit's gala opening at the Fernand et Fils gallery. My artist has agreed to accompany me to the dinner. He feels that it will be a welcome distraction. I do too. We are both on tenterhooks about the reception he will receive on this, his third *vernissage*.

If Brit and I are on tenterhooks, so are Jean-Luc – the *chef* – and his beloved Isabella. He has definitely decided on *Boeuf Bourguignon* as the main course (partly because he has discovered that it is a favorite of Monsieur Dupris, from the office of the President of France, who has reserved a place with his wife for the dinner). For *entrée*, smoked Scotch salmon on blinis with sour cream, and elegant, light *meringues* with macerated berries (macerated in *framboise*) with *crème fraiche* to finish.

Oh the shopping. Finding the very best. Then, the early preparations: the whipping of the egg whites for the *meringues* and the slow cooking until they are perfection; the peeling of the small white onions for the *boeuf* dish, the mushrooms, the braising of the meat; the selection of the perfect burgundy.

Brit and I are participants in some of this, as excited as our delightful hotelier. Brit particularly enjoys the selection of the wine. "We must find something to impress not only Monsieur Dupris, but our friend, the new vintner, Franco de Peverelli…something to inspire him."

On the Saturday, two days before the Hotel Marcel Dining Club experience, Jean-Luc, Brit, and I are in pursuit of the perfect bottle (bottles). A burgundy, of course. As it is a true *Boeuf Bourguignon,* it will be used in the cookery, as well as drunk at table. "It has to be of the highest quality," Jean-Luc insists, and we head off to his favorite wine merchant who has a shop in the 10th *arrondissement.*

The wine shop is all the way across town. It is a bright, cold November day, and Brit and I are pleased to be part of the search. Also we just might learn something.

The three of us arrive in Brit's Peugeot at a small storefront with a large sign: "Leon Chauffade…*Maître des Vins.*" As we enter, I am struck by how unlikely a wine merchant Monsieur Chauffade appears to be. He is small, birdlike, but with a radiant smile and a red nose. He greets Jean-Luc with warmth.

They embrace, pat each other's backs and in rapid French, discuss the problem at hand. "It has to be special, this wine," Jean-Luc suddenly says in English, turning to us as we peer about the room with shelves to the ceiling, each loaded with rows of bottles. It is mind-boggling.

How can one possibly choose?

"For a *Boeuf Bourguignon,* such as you will cook," Monsieur Chauffade begins, "of course you will need a full-bodied burgundy." His English is surprisingly good. "I have several from the Côte d'Or," he continues, going behind the counter. "There is the *Chambertin*…hmm, and the *Fleurie*…but no, no, too summery…an excellent red when chilled on a hot day…and then there's the *Volnay*…I think too soft and delicate for a braised beef such as you are going to create."

"Yes, yes," says Jean-Luc, with growing impatience. "I want something big…full-bodied."

"I have it, *mon ami.* Just the thing. It is also from the Côte d'Or. A *Vosne-Romanée.* Perfect! It has to be at least five years old to be developed in full flavor…but I have plenty in stock."

Brit and I have been wandering about the small store, marveling at the enormous numbers of names and areas – from Bordeaux to Burgundy, from Alsace and the Loire Valley. All France is represented here in the form of liquid pleasure done up in a bottle.

By this time, Jean-Luc has purchased eight of the *Vosne-Romanée.* Brit laughs. "You think that's enough?"

"You know? I think not. I'll take another two, Leon," he says to the little wine-master.

Then to Brit, "I'll need at least two bottles to 'please' the *boeuf…*"

"And a bottle for every single person at the table?" Brit asks in mock horror.

"Hey," Jean-Luc responds. You never know. Besides, Isabella and I might enjoy a glass or two if there is any left over, but mark my words. There won't be."

CHAPTER 19

Saki

SUNDAY MORNING, BRIT and I, with Giscard, finish crating the last pictures and bringing them to Fernand et Fils. We leave them in the storage room at the rear of the building, returning after 5:00 o'clock.

Monsieur Fernand closes the gallery, so Brit, Giscard and I can work for a few hours, mounting Brit's show, *Les Peintures Lumineuses,* opening Tuesday, November 10th. After toiling some hours, we stop for a quick *omelette au fromage,* and several glasses of *Pinot Noir* at *La Terrasse,* a bistro near the Hotel Marcel. It is then to bed, exhausted.

The work at the gallery continues on Monday as well. The place is closed that day, Monday being a general day of rest for the tradesmen of Paris.

Giscard pitches in and is full of inspiration. He is an accomplished workman, metals, anvils, and hammers his modus operandi. However, he also has something of an artist's eye.

"It's all in perception," he remarks. Brit is, in spite of himself, impressed and truly grateful.

I am along for the ride and thoroughly enjoying myself, glad to be part of the pre-process for the show. I am busy labeling the paintings as they are hung, distributing brochure material about the two main rooms, and stapling lists of prices strategically.

The two men are into the heavy work of lifting and hanging, deciding space and rapport between the pictures. Equally, they are intent on preparing the lighting, so important for the display. Monsieur Fernand appears from time to time to nod approval or shake his head. "*Non, non,* too close to the lavatory."

We break for lunch. Nearby is *Sushi Paris* where we partake of tepid tempura and sushi rolls. Also saki. Not bad. Not bad at all.

And on returning to our labor of love, we are more compatible as a threesome, more filled with laughter and excitement because the *vernissage* is shaping up to be a thing of beauty, the paintings dramatic and intense in their placement under discreet beams of light.

The saki helps.

CHAPTER 20

Beef Stew

JEAN-LUC IS EXCITED about his menu for the second Hotel Marcel Dining Club. With any number of possibilities, he decides that, *au fond*, a dish so intrinsically French, as the classic *Boeuf Bourguignon* will be most appreciated.

He decided on the date, November 9th, the Monday evening before Brit's *vernissage* at the Fernand et Fils gallery because "as my second adventure in the world of the *chef*, and although it has only been one week since the first, I feel I must 'strike while the irons are hot', as they say in English, no?" he exclaims. I nod with a smile.

So for the *Cercle Privé*, the dinner set for the evening of November 9th at 8:00 PM, he prepares the *entrée* over a period of two days, at his Cornu stove in his apartment across the street from the hotel. He also bakes the small elegant *meringues*, for the *Meringues Chantilly* dessert.

Jean-Luc is particularly pleased with his true-French menu selection because a very important assistant to the President of France, François Hollande - a Monsieur and Madame Dupris - have reserved to enjoy the exceptional dinner *chez* Hotel Marcel. His *Cercle Privé* is certainly becoming exclusive and important if such a political figure and his spouse plan to attend.

On the late afternoon of the event in question, Willie Blakely is carrying a large, covered cast iron pot with a long handle, filled with *Boeuf Bourguignon,* the tiny Ana Wi following him with a basket of *meringues,* wrapped in a cloth, a bowl of berries macerated in orange *liqueur,* and a cold bowl of *crème fraiche.* She also has in her basket small blinis and smoked salmon from Scotland with sour cream and lemons in separate containers.

Willie's pot is redolent of burgundy wine, with a hint of garlic and bay leaf, bacon and onion, the aroma of which wafts above the smell of auto exhaust and city traffic, as he crosses from one side of the street to the other, his assistant behind him.

He is deft at dodging the cars, and Ana Wi follows his quick steps like his shadow. He does not notice, as they reach the entrance to the Hotel Marcel, that Ana Wi, now next to him, is struggling to lift the cover of the pot he carries just slightly, with her free hand. He thinks she is merely trying to help him carry the heavy load.

The second *diner* of The Hotel Marcel Dining Club, By Invitation Only, has arrived at its destination – the little back kitchen at the rear of the hotel building. The huge pot of *Boeuf Bourguignon* is placed upon the two back burners of the stove to keep it hot and fragrant. Ana Wi, disgruntled by her failed attempt, places her dessert and appetizer items on the small counter, the *crème fraiche* and berries in the small refrigerator. She then starts to leave for the salon, preparing to set the table for eight people.

Willie gives her a glance, concerned at her sour expression. "Is something wrong, *ma cherie?*" he inquires.

"*Rien,* Willie. It's nothing," and she goes about her business. He follows her movements. Something in her manner is surly, so different. He is disturbed.

It is fortunate that Willie guards the large pot of *Boeuf Bourguignon* on the stove burners, for Ana Wi keeps trying to look into the pot, to poke at it (in truth to poison it), but Willie, all innocence, guards it carefully and instructs his small Asian assistant to do her duties in the salon.

The guests have assembled. Frank Sinatra sings the lovely "April in Paris" softly through Jean-Luc's speaker system.

This evening, the eight include Circy Detweiler and her consort, Dr. Guillaume Paxière. (Again. She finds The Hotel Marcel Dining Club irresistible and so exclusive.) Also at table, of all people, Jerry and Madge, the American couple from the state of Georgia who, on returning to the states, will report on how they were participants in an elite Private Circle dining experience, 'By Invitation Only', although, later, quite frankly, they are disappointed in this evening's menu. "Beef stew?" Jerry whispers to Madge, with a sniff.

Above all others, there is the French political couple from the office of the President of France, Monsieur and Madame Dupris. They contribute little at first, however their looks are glossy and expensive, if a bit forbidding. Jean-Luc is proud to have them among the assembled guests. He is very deferential to them, and although they appear quite formal, it is evident they find the *plats* before them exceptional. They seem to relax into a companionable enjoyment as the dinner progresses.

Finally there is Brit and me. I will be leaving for home the end of the week, so it is my last opportunity to share in The Hotel Marcel Dining Club experience, only the second to have taken place – until I return in the spring.

We are indulging in the delicate, rosy smoked salmon on small blinis, with sour cream as garnish, when I hear a ruckus in the kitchen at the rear of the salon. There is the sound of raised voices – a man and a woman, both in English: the man, 'what do you think you're doing?' and the high voice of the woman, 'nothing sir. I am just stirring the pot.' 'That's not what it looks like to me!' is his muttered reply.

Is that Giscard Poignal's voice? Why and how did he get back there?

There is silence at our table, as Jean-Luc strides the length of the room and enters the kitchen, shutting the door behind him, but this, of course, does not stop the angry voices from reaching the ears of the diners who pause, looking from one to the other, over the elegant salmon appetizer. There is now a third voice: Jean-Luc's.

His tone is lower and I can hear the sputter in it. 'What is going on?' and she, 'nothing sir...nothing' and then the second male voice, (it IS Giscard's), 'I think she is trying to put something in the pot,' and then Jean-Luc, with an explosive 'what?'

Willie, who has been opening bottles of burgundy wine in the salon, rushes back to the kitchen. He recognizes the woman's voice: his Ana Wi.

"Get out, Madame," I hear Jean-Luc say in his most commanding manner. "Get out now. I will deal with you later." There is a shuffling noise, a slammed door, and immediately, Jean-Luc pokes his head into the room and says blithely to us, *"Pas de problème, Messieurs, Mesdames. Un moment."* And his head disappears.

Isabella at the front of the salon has taken Willie's role of refilling the flutes with *champagne* and smiling mightily. We resume our delectation, and I hear distinct sounds of contentment, even delight, over the delicious *plat*. In fact, there is nothing to be said as all eight of us truly relish the exquisite appetizer. Willie has returned to clear the plates and place small baskets of *mini-baguettes* in front of each place setting – *"pour la sauce"* he whispers to each of us. He also puts a second wine glass for each, and proceeds to present to Monsieur Dupris, an opened (to breathe) bottle of burgundy for his perusal.

"It is a *Vosne Romanée*, from the Côte d'Or, a great burgundy, Monsieur. Please notice the date."

"I see, I see," Monsieur Dupris says, as he puts on his glasses and inspects the bottle carefully. "Excellent."

Madame Dupris, who, up to now, has said little, except to her husband, asks Willie, "Just what is the *pièce de résistance?*"

"Madame, it is the *classique Boeuf Bourguignon.*"

"Bon," interjects Monsieur Dupris, tucking his napkin above his weskit. "I love the true French traditions. This is one of my favorites," and with this remark, the ice at the table is broken and an animated conversation flows. That is until the *pièce de résistance* appears in all its

delicious glory, and then talking ceases and a focused eating takes place with only the sound of the contented sigh.

By the time the beautiful *meringues* with macerated berries and *crème fraiche* arrive, we are all in a lovely haze. Jean-Luc still stands proudly at the front of the room. Giscard Poignal has entered to stand beside him, observing us as we devour the light and ethereal dessert, sip the black espressos, touched with a hint of good *Armangac*.

On leaving, Monsieur and Madame Dupris approach their host, and with a resounding slap on the back, Dupris says to Jean-Luc. "Well done, Monsieur. We will surely be back. And I will tell my colleagues of this most French and totally satisfying dining experience. I wish you *bon nuit*." With that, he takes his wife's arm, and with a little bow, leaves the premises.

After Madge and Jerry leave quite unceremoniously, and Circy with her doctor depart, Brit and I approach Jean-Luc and Giscard, both of whom are now sitting on the sofa in the lounge area. Willie and Isabella are on kitchen duty, shorthanded because of Ana Wi's dismissal.

"What in heaven's name happened back there?" Brit asks.

"That little woman was trying to poison the pot, that's what happened," Jean-Luc says through clenched teeth. "Can you imagine?"

"You're kidding," I say.

"I wish he was," says Giscard. "But I saw it. She has a handful of some noxious looking straw bits and even something that looked like it wiggled. I couldn't believe it. It was disgusting!"

"*Dégoutant!*" repeats Jean-Luc.

"Indeed, *dégoutant*," says a woeful looking Willie who has come to stand before us. "I am so sorry, Monsieur Marcel. So sorry. I dunno what to do." Willie really is pale and shaken.

"It's not your fault, old friend," says Jean-Luc. "Who could have known that that quiet, little inscrutable woman could do such mischief!"

"Inscrutable is the operative word," Giscard interjects. "And I have to tell you Willie – and I know it will hurt – but I have heard – next door – that Yoki Atari and Ana..."

"Say no more, sir," says Willie hurriedly, and in a low tone says, "I get the message," and he turns on his heel and leaves quickly. There is silence and then I say, "I feel so sorry for Willie. He doesn't deserve this."

"Just who does deserve betrayal?" Giscard remarks slowly. I find his words ironic.

"How do you intend to handle this, Jean-Luc?" Brit asks. "It's no laughing matter."

"It surely isn't" is his reply. "The first thing is my call to your brother," he says to Giscard, as he rises to go to his office. "René, *bien sûr*," Jean-Luc says firmly to himself as he leaves us clustered there in a worried little group.

CHAPTER 21

Les Peintures Lumineuses

LUMINOUS IMAGES. PICTURES filled with light. This is Brit's show – Ludwig Turner, my artist lover/friend and master painter. How proud I am, on this Tuesday evening, November 10th. It is near 5:30 and the gallery, Fernand et Fils, on the rue St. Honoré is filling rapidly with art enthusiasts and critics, collectors and friends.

Les Peintures Lumineuses. This is the title of the exhibition, which will run until Christmas. There are 28 paintings in all, some large, others smaller, with a sheaf of drawings and sketches in a case by the front door. Brit stands beside it, with Fernand, Sr., the owner of the esteemed gallery, greeting the individuals who enter, directing them toward the two inner rooms.

One of the rooms is darkened, the farthest of the inner rooms. Giscard's creative efforts on my Brit's behalf are sensational. He has welded together strips of metal, framing not one but two large paintings, back to back, supported the whole from a wire in the ceiling of the gallery room that somehow makes the pair rotate. Meanwhile, in the center of the darkened gallery room, the images are lighted – at times with flickering rays – to produce the most unusual and thrilling effect. Brit is beside himself with the result.

"It's beyond anything I have ever seen – and how exquisitely the paintings present themselves." Brit is shaking his head in wonder. "Dammit, Giscard! You've given my work a whole new dimension."

The three of us stand before this mounting in awe. Although Brit has always held reservations about Giscard, at least in terms of his lascivious behavior (and flirtatious talk with me), his admiration for Giscard's prowess in his chosen field, - welding – (not sex) – Brit has to admire.

And he is thankful. After all, how tremendous the paintings are displayed. How strong an impact they produce in the eye of the beholder.

We return to the center room where young boys with white aprons, tied at the waist reaching the floor, pass champagne *flutes*, while three pretty waitresses pass warm *gougères* and trays of *foie gras* on toast. How delectable. For November, the *crépuscule* – the twilight - is warm, the front door to the gallery wide open.

I will be leaving Paris in a few days. This night is the height of my visit. How handsome Brit looks! How animated and proud is his demeanor, not at all arrogant but sure of himself and of the quality of the images he has created.

There's Circy, I see, and the ever present Dr. Guillaume Paxière. I can tell he is combing the room for new sexual prey, much to Circy's dismay. She keeps tugging his sleeve, shaking her head.

Jean-Luc and Isabella are among the crowd, as is Sue de Chevigny. She is standing with Franco de Peverelli, in one corner of the center room, enthralled by a large abstract in brilliant colors of red and orange, with deep black lines and blocks of purple. As I approach, I hear her say to him, "It's stunning! It would be so exciting in the library – with all its dark wood. It would enliven the place..."

"Indeed it would," Franco remarks. "Hmm. It also might be a dramatic image for a label for the wine bottles...'Le Couvent'! I can see the winery's name emblazoned on that brilliant color. What do you think, *cherie?*"

"I think it is you who are brilliant! What a grand idea. Ah, Elizabeth. Did you hear? Don't you think it would be marvelous for our bottles?"

"You have to buy it first," I say with a laugh.

"Of course. Of course," the two say, joining me in merriment. "Of course we'll purchase it. And how beautiful it will be in the library of the *château*."

Franco adds, "And Sue, perhaps as cover for our wine cookbook!"

"What a great idea - you're writing a cookbook!" I exclaim. "I love it!"

"Yes indeed," says Sue. "Cooking with wine – of course – with OUR wine. *'Le Couvent Cave à Vin'* – that's the title – with the subtitle – *Le Couvent à Table.*"

"*Cave à Vin?*" I question.

"It means wine cellar," Sue says dismissively. "And of course, '*à Table*' means just what it says – at the table – *à manger.*"

"Okay, okay, you two", Jean-Luc interjects. "The painting is quite *magnifique.*" Isabella has approached it, inspecting it closely. "I don't know how Brit manages to meld the colors. They are so strong, but somehow, he makes the pigments work together in quite an astonishing way." I can tell, as an artist herself in the world of fabric and design, she is impressed.

When uh-oh. Here comes Circy with a nasty expression on her face. She is moving quickly towards Isabella and in her high, penetrating voice, accosts the young woman, actually poking her on the shoulder. Isabella steps back.

"So it is you – you personally – who have decided against Yves St. Laurent displaying and merchandising my perfumes and colognes!"

"*Pardon?*" Isabella is stunned.

"I was told by that officious Madame Generet, at your office, that YOU had decided my product was not good enough to be traded by St. Laurent." Circy is weaving a little. Too much *champagne?*

"Madame," Isabella says with dignity. "It was not my decision alone, I can assure you. We felt that your...concoctions were perhaps too... exotic...the idea of herbs as a basis for scents...although it is a most original concept, it is not quite appropriate for our market."

"That's ridiculous! It's appropriate – as you call it – for ANY market – not just your snobby, French…"

"Please, Circy," Guillaume Paxière says. He appears to be totally embarrassed. This is not the kind of scene the good doctor appreciates.

It is at that moment that Giscard Poignal appears from the innermost room. Circy Detweiler's face changes expression like lightening. I believe she has never encountered quite such a seductive looking man, and as her mouth slightly opens, and her cheeks turn rosy, she blurts out, "Now who is this?"

"Giscard Poignal, at your service, Madame," he says with that bewitching smile. (Really, Giscard! You are something else!) I can see Guillaume bristle. This is becoming quite funny. Somehow, Giscard Poignal, René's younger brother has saved the day. Circy is completely defanged!

Most important of all, Giscard has caused for Brit a tremendous interest in the presentation of the 'Double Painting' in the inner room. It turns out that *'tout Paris'* buzzes about it for the next days. "A New Way of Seeing" are words describing the dimension of the 'Double Painting.' *"Unique et Nouveau"* is the title of one review of Brit's work. Ludwig Turner is the new darling of the Paris world of art.

CHAPTER 22

A Welcome Invitation

SUE HAS INVITED Brit and me to *Le Couvent* for the Wednesday and Thursday nights before my departure next weekend on Saturday, November 14th. We are delighted to accept. Brit is exhausted from the frantic work preparing for his show. The two-day respite in the embrace of such dear friends as Sue and Franco cannot be anything but restortive, in every regard. I cannot wait to find out more about the cookbook. I can't wait to taste the new *Le Couvent* wines. And I can't wait to be in one of the astonishingly small beds in the upper gallery of the old *château* with Brit in my arms.

Before Brit and I leave for Montoire Wednesday morning, I step out on the balcony off my Hotel Marcel bedroom. It is a crisp and clear November day. I view the familiar apartments across the street, and suddenly, I see, leaving the huge front door of The Majestic next door, René Poignal. He is escorting, in handcuffs, not one, but two people. Ana Wi and Yoki Atari. Both of their heads are bowed. Nelson stands in the doorway, all puffed up and red in the face. This is not the first time I have seen the arrests of mal-doers by one intrepid detective, René Poignal.

I call to Brit who joins me on the balcony in his bathrobe, and we wait, watching until the police car's braying siren starts and the automobile pulls away.

"Done and done," he says.

"Thank God", I respond, with a sigh.

Brit and I drive down to *Le Couvent* in the Peugeot on this Wednesday morning. There is a slight haze. It is a leisurely couple of hours we spend, saying little, except to agree that Jean-Luc and the clientele for The Hotel Marcel Dining Club are considerably safer now that the two 'criminals' were taken into custody by René Poignal.

We listen to Charles Trenet – the French crooner from the 1950s – on the radio. Brit loves this station. It has all the old, golden songs from that period – Edith Piaf, Yves Montand – even Maurice Chevalier. "Bonjour, Jolie Madame," Trenet sings in his lovely, lilting bass voice, and I look at Brit and marvel at my own happiness.

Our two friends are waiting for us at the front door of the *château*. After embraces, and warm greetings, we repair to the kitchen downstairs to a lunch prepared by Franco using of course, his latest wine pressing in the braise.

The dish is Franco's *Coq au Riesling* – not really using the actual *Riesling*, the German wine – but a white wine of similar lightness and fruitiness, taken from the grapes from the hills our host/chef has personally terraced at the rear of the *château*. Sue had mentioned the dish at *Le Chêne*. I can't wait to taste it.

The chicken, *sautéed* until brown, then braised with thyme, a hint of garlic, some pale mushrooms, in a goodly amount of the light white wine, and at the end, jolted with a shot of both *cognac* and heavy cream, was ethereal and delectable.

"One for '*Le Couvent Cave à Vin*' - that's the name of your cookbook, no?" remarks Brit, lapping up the last bit of sauce with a crusty piece of *baguette*.

"So this is *'Le Couvent à Table!'* I say, "in all its glory. I love it. And SO good. Absolutely spectacular."

"Not as spectacular as your show last night, Monsieur Brit. You should be congratulated."

"I have to say I'm pleased," Brit says, leaning back, not in the least smug. "It makes me want to work more." He puts his head down.

"Now don't be coy, Brit," Sue says with a little laugh. "You deserve tremendous credit…"

"Well, quite honestly, so does Giscard Poignal. His mounting…"

"The Double Painting?" Franco asks.

"Yes, that. It was inspired. And it was all his idea."

"But he did not create the pictures, Brit," I say solemnly. "That is you. Your artistry. It is your gift that people are raving about."

He shoots me a grateful glance. "There is one thing about Giscard, though, that bothers me."

"His reputation?" says Sue with a raised eyebrow and small smile.

"Well, I guess there's that," Brit says, "although he's surely not the only *roué* in all of Paris."

"I should say not," says Franco with a laugh.

"What bothers you about him?" Sue asks.

"Well…at the *vernissage*, he really behaved quite heroically with Circy… right in the middle of everything, I told him how grateful I was for his help in mounting the show…that I thought he deserved a reward."

"You did?" I am surprised.

"He turned to me," Brit went on, not looking at me, "I want the picture of the woman…"

"Which picture?" I say, alarmed.

"The one I painted of you – you know the barely seen woman from the back…lying on a divan…as through a mist… creamy…"

Sue is looking at us back and forth as at a tennis game. "He painted you nude?" She has a twinkle in her eye.

"It's kind of personal," I say, blushing.

"I paint with a pointillist's touch…" Brit interjects, trying to save the situation.

"Pointillist?" Sue questions. "Tiny dots?"

"More like specks of light and color, one after the other, to create… someone …light, color, luminous passion…but for me, in the abstract."

"Okay, okay," I say with a laugh.

"Giscard saw…even though abstract…he saw…you," Brit says, turning to me.

There is a moment of no conversation.

"Anyway," Brit continues, "Giscard wanted it. He almost demanded it. I was speechless. Then he said, 'I would take your woman if I could… but I know I can't.'"

I realize I am quite flushed. I also realize Brit is looking at me with a kind of distrust. Can he be jealous? It's ridiculous.

We go upstairs to the small bed, so characteristic of these older *châteaux* (earlier lords and ladies were smaller than those of this century) to prepare for a nap. Brit lies with his back to me. It is so unlike his usual demeanor with me that I rise and decide to go downstairs.

I find our hostess, Sue, sitting in the little alcove off the great salon. She is trying to write her memoir – "for the kids," she says. Her three children are all married and living about Europe. "They always wonder where I've been and why. 'You were in Istanbul? Why, *Maman?*' or 'When did you and Papa decide to take horse *dressage?*' By the way, that's a wonderful hobby. Paul and I had such fun…" she continues. "But you. You look woeful? What's up?"

"I don't know. Brit seems to be kind of mad at me – irritated for some reason. I don't know what I've done."

Sue starts to giggle. "Sweetheart, he's jealous."

"Jealous? Of whom?"

"Giscard, of course."

"That's absurd!"

"No. I've noticed. It isn't anything you've provoked. It's the 'bad boy' himself. He has the 'hots' for you…"

"Oh come on. That's just silly."

"No. I don't mean to be crass, but he has the 'hots' for any attractive woman…even me. He can't help it. But Brit? Well, he is possessive of you – which is great – and at the same time, he's threatened by Giscard's... charms? After all, that smile of his..."

With this, I begin to relax. "I tell you what," Sue goes on. "I have an idea. Come with me," and we descend to the kitchen.

She brings out pounds of butter – the sweet French butter from Brittany. She takes cups of flour from a canister, and a sack of sugar, also a small bottle of vanilla extract. In a bowl, she creates a dough from these simple ingredients, rolls it out, cuts it up, and proceeds to bake the cookies in a 350 degree oven for a little over 10 minutes. When done, she sprinkles them with sugar.

"Taste this, Elizabeth," my American Marquise demands, holding out a warm cookie from the tray. I do, and I can't believe how crumbly sweet is this shortbread just created, truly delectable.

"Tell Brit you cooked these just for him! I guarantee, he will be completely placated. Believe me," she says with a sly wink. "It works."

When I return upstairs with my prize, I find a tousled Brit, awake and restless on the narrow bed. "Here. I made something for you," I say with my most beguiling smile. As he eats the cookie, crumbles falling onto the sheet, I see his face light up with delight.

"These are incredible. You made these?" I nod demurely.

"For me?"

"Just for you, Brit. Just for you."

And Sue is right. It works.

CHAPTER 23

A Visitor

SUE HAS AN unexpected surprise for Brit and me, this Thursday at the *château, Le Couvent,* in Montoire. A black town car arrives about noon, and out steps Henri Bresson in a tightly belted trench coat, a small hat on his head.

"I forgot to tell you," she says quickly with a smile, as she moves forward to greet the new guest on the large stoop in front of the grand door of the *château.*

"Please come in, Monsieur," she says. "Welcome to *Le Couvent,*" and she takes him by the arm, receives his hat which he proffers, and they enter the foyer.

"You have a most beautiful property, Madame," Henri Bresson says. "I am delighted to be here."

"We are indeed pleased to have you," Sue responds, as Franco joins her, and the three enter the grand salon where Brit and I are standing by the fireplace. "Just wait until you see the vineyard."

"Yes," Franco interjects. "I want to show you my terraced plants to the rear of the *château*."

"It is Franco's pride and joy," Sue says beaming.

Henri Bresson is nodding, smiling. He is not known for small talk, but one can see he is genuinely pleased with his surroundings. For a Frenchman from a small town in the Auvergne, a *château*, a *Marquise*, a now well-known artist (Brit), well, these are a step up in his world. It just depends on the *cuisine*, cooked in home-pressed wine, that, for the food critic, will be the test.

Franco whisks Henri Bresson off to view his handiwork on the hills of wine grapes. Sue takes Brit and me into the small dining room off the upstairs kitchen (which she rarely uses, preferring the old equipment in the stone room in the basement). The table is set for the five of us with white linen, her best china and silverware.

"Franco has made a superb *Ossobuco*. It's resting downstairs...veal shanks he cooked in his best white wine. He used bottles of *Vernaccia* – the great white from his home in Tuscany. But of course, the grapes for it are now grown here from the seedlings he brought to *Le Couvent*."

"Illegally," Brit says with a grin.

"Of course illegally, but who cares? Not me. Not René Poignal, and after tasting it, not Henri Bresson. We are having it poured at table, as well, with the *Ossobuco*."

I can't wait." And I can't.

"We are hoping..." Sue says, somewhat agitated, "that Monsieur Bresson will write a forward to our cookbook. I am praying he will be impressed enough...although the *Vernaccia* – made here – is almost as great as the Tuscany pressing – but not quite. Still, Franco is pleased that it 'translated' from Italy to France as well as it did. He is quite proud of it."

"I'll bet Henri Bresson will be impressed with it too," I say.

The two men return, flushed, animated, and we are served an *apéritif* of a sweet vermouth on ice "pressed only recently" Franco quickly explains.

"This is good," says Brit appreciatively, sipping the icy drink slowly. Toasted almonds and black *Niçoise* olives are passed by Francine, the *femme de chambre* at *Le Couvent,* the only servant Sue can afford (yet).

As we sit at our places at table, Franco waxes eloquent in describing his efforts at creating the *Le Couvent* vineyard and winery. As he pours the *Vernaccia,* slightly chilled, into each of our wine glasses, he says, "*naturellement,* in another year this wine's grapes will be in their prime!"

Is this a semi-apology, I wonder, or is it to prepare the famous food critic for a less than perfect wondrous bouquet and flavor to our libation.

Then, Franco goes into detail about the cookbook he and the Marquise are writing together, explaining that all of the recipes will involve wine, from the great braising dishes, to poached fruit, even to pickling and preserving.

"A most interesting concept," Henri was saying. "I don't know of another such book with a total wine emphasis."

The large, red *Le Creuset* casserole is presented at Franco's end of the table. Warm plates are put before him, and he proceeds gracefully, and with a good amount of pride, to ladle out the fragrant *Ossobuco* onto plates which Francine places before each of us.

The veal shanks are tender and flavorful. The sauce with thyme, a hint of garlic and lemon, and the slightly fruity *Vernaccia,* is elegant and just light enough to coat the meat and its succulent marrow.

Wow," is Brit's comment.

Henri remains silent but he eats every scrap and sops up the sauce with *baguette.* After a simple, lettuce salad, a bit of cheese, there is dessert.

What else?

Pears poached in red wine from the hills of *Le Couvent!*

CHAPTER 24

A Last Supper

I LEAVE TOMORROW. *Demain!* The word in French has such a sad ring.

For my final dinner this Friday, my last evening in Paris, at the delightful *Caviar Kaspia* on the Place Madeleine on the Right Bank, there are Jean-Luc and Isabella, La Marquise Sue de Chevigny with Franco de Peverelli, Brit and me.

Brit had even asked Giscard Poignal to join us. "I feel I owe him," he tells me, "for all he did to help me with the show."

"You could have rewarded him with the picture of my nude backside," I say with a sly smile.

"You must be kidding!" Brit exclaims. "Anyway, he told me he was going to a concert Friday night – a rock band from America called of all things, 'Eagles of Death Metal.'"

"I've heard of them," I respond. "I didn't know Giscard was so... well... 'mod'."

"I guess we don't know all that much about Giscard – except that he's been something of a hero more than once."

"Where's the concert? Is he taking someone...female?"

Brit laughs. "That I don't know. But if not, he'll surely find one there."

"*Sans doute, sans doute*," Jean-Luc echoes.

"The concert is over somewhere near La Place de la République, I understand," Brit continues.

"Sue and I had lunch over there last week. Interesting area," I add.

We sip our drinks in the upstairs room at *Caviar Kaspia* this Friday evening, awaiting the *entrées* to come. I have ordered, *naturellement*, my favorite dish in all the world, the baked potato, fluffed high with sour cream and butter, and topped with beluga caviar. (It is excellent with salmon roe as well.)

I notice Henri Bresson in a corner by the window overlooking La Place Madeleine. I am sure he already knows this dining room, the *chef*, the management, because he has already reviewed (magnificently) this revered emporium of delicacies from the sea. He is with a charming looking woman.

"There's our food critic," I whisper surreptitiously to Isabella. "I wonder who's his date?"

With a quick look, Isabella says, "Oh, she's a well-known hostess/ philanthropist. I believe her name is Jacqueline de Moroncy."

"Only the best for our Henri Bresson," I say. "He was down for lunch with us yesterday at *Le Couvent*."

Isabella laughs. "He does get around in the highest circles, no?"

Brit is telling Jean-Luc of the vision of René marching off with Ana Wi and Yoki Atari we had glimpsed from the balcony on the 5th floor last Wednesday morning. "It was quite a sight to see the two, so subdued, with hands in cuffs behind their backs."

"Yes, yes," Jean-Luc says, "a welcome ending to the whole business. It could have made a *désastre* for my Dining Club."

"Well, a disaster it wasn't thanks to Giscard Poignal being at the right place at the right time. He caught Ana Wi in the act."

"*Merci à Dieu*," says Jean-Luc, making a small cross with his finger over his chest.

"Yes indeed," I say. "Thank God," I reiterate in English."

"It was so lucky that Giscard was there exactly when she was doctoring the pot," Brit says.

"Lucky?" I question. "Just how come did he happen to be in the little kitchen of the hotel on such a grand important evening? Nobody ever goes back there."

"He was there," Jean-Luc says, "because he has a small habit. He keeps a bottle of vodka in my icebox…in the freezer, if you can imagine, a trick he learned in America. He goes there when he wants a shot."

"He was thirsty," I say with a grin. "How fortunate."

"Thank God he was thirsty," Jean-Luc says, reaffirming my remark.

"And by the way, I am thirsty too. Let's get another carafe of that very 'fortunate' liquor, shall we?"

And we do.

"Giscard is something of a hero," I say, at which Brit shoots me a look. "Well he is," I say defensively. "He spotted Ana, didn't he? And don't forget, he seduced and defeated my nemesis, Bonny Brandeis, last year, when she tried to steal my identity, credit cards, money – leaving me broke. He made her fall in love with him and then left her at the altar."

Brit is still looking at me.

"Well, it's true, Brit. Give the devil his due."

"Oh, I do," he replies. "René's younger brother, the renegade and rogue, the 'bad boy', '*mauvais fils*', I agree, he is a hero. Look what he did for my art exhibition. He gave it the extra step."

Jean-Luc, watching this interplay, to change the subject, suddenly remarks, "You know, I think I may ask other *chefs* – the good ones, of course, to create their specialties for my Hotel Marcel Dining Club. What do you think?" He addresses this to Franco.

"Why would you do this?" I interrupt before Franco can respond, thankful that Giscard is no longer the subject.

"I think perhaps it would make the dinners more interesting," Jean-Luc expounds. "*Par exemple*, Antonio Giovanni from *di Felice* – you know, the restaurant on rue de Grenelle. He could make his superb, authentic Italian *lasagna* for a particular evening – or *chef* Georges Benoit of the *Bellehara* could create his *ris de veau*, the sweetbreads you love so much, Elizabeth."

"Oh, Monsieur Benoit! His *ris* are divine…so earthy…braised with a little crust."

"His specialty is offal – the innards. He is the best at their preparation – liver with caramelized onions and bacon - and kidneys in a mustard sauce – *superbe*."

"I love the innards," I say, and for some reason, everyone laughs.

"You mustn't laugh," says Jean-Luc, trying to control his own. "Offal is interesting. The French nobles threw away the offal to the peasants. Not fit to eat. The peasants in turn, created some of the greatest *cuisine* of France, by braising, in wine and herbs, sweet butter, bacon – in due course, the aristocracy took these masterpieces of cookery to its breast as if it was its own."

While we are devouring our caviar, the beads of which pop on the tongue, and unctuous smoked salmon on toast, and crabmeat with a sauce *remoulade*, during this repast, suddenly Franco pipes up with a question to Jean-Luc.

"Monsieur Marcel, do you think it possible that I might be a guest *chef* one night…?"

Sue looks surprised, but interjects, "You know Jean-Luc, Franco has created some truly delicious dishes with our own wine. It would be such fun if he could have one evening at your hotel *Cercle Privé* dinner." She looks at Jean-Luc beseechingly.

"*Peut-être*, Madame, if I like his cooking," he says with a grin.

"You will. You will," she says happily.

When we descend the stairs of *Caviar Kaspia*, passing the cold cases of smoked salmon and beluga caviar in the shop on the ground floor – when we reach the street, I am struck by the silence of the city. It feels like it is in mourning for my departure tomorrow. There seems to be a pall over the usually busy Place de la Madeleine. It is as if time has frozen.

The old Peugeot delivers me to the Hotel Marcel, this, my final night, and there, I clasp Brit to me like there is no tomorrow.

And in fact, on rising on the morning of November 14th, 2015, there is no tomorrow for so many in Paris, after the night of the assassins. No tomorrow at all.

CHAPTER 25

A New Planet

"THAT'S WHAT PARIS is. A new planet," Jean-Luc says sadly with a shrug of his shoulders. "We are all in mourning. We are living with it now."

I sit in the salon at the table, Brit holding my hand, on this Saturday, November 14, 2015. In a little while, he will drive me to Charles de Gaulle to fly home.

"Tranquility lost," murmurs Ray Guild. He is sitting at the table over a cup of *café au lait*. He has come to say his goodbye to me as I prepare myself for untold delays at the airport on my way back to the States. René Poignal has joined us.

"I think we are all afflicted by guilt," he says in his policeman's voice.

"Guilt?" I ask. "Why should we feel guilt?"

"Because we survive," is his blunt answer. And he's right. There is a terrible sense of self-reproach, a nameless culpability. Yet with all the sadness, the people of Paris retain a fierce realism.

And Giscard. He was going to the concert at *Le Bataclan* last night where terrible carnage occurred, according to reports on television. I dare to ask the good detective, "Giscard? You've heard from him?" I say it timorously.

René nods. "He's okay, but in pretty bad shape. Says it was horrible – unbelievably cruel. He said they…the men with guns…were laughing." René bows his head. There are tears in his eyes. They do not fall.

I am not surprised at his tears. This desecration of Paris and its way of life is beyond anything any of us has experienced. We are numb.

René has always seemed so resolute, so professional. How many times have I seen him cart people off to jail. It seems, every time I am in Paris, there is some crime for him to solve.

I saw him drag off Kurt Vronsky, the brute who murdered his brother-in-law in apartment building number one; I remember him arresting Gillian Spenser, the copyist of great artists' paintings which she fraudulently sold; and there was Ahmed, Hamad al-Boudi's arsonist minion who tried to burn down the Hotel Marcel; and only last year, it was Bonny Brandeis, on her 'wedding' day, René cuffed and led off to jail.

This trip, it is Ana Wi, for attempting to poison Jean-Luc's *Boeuf Bourguignon*, and Yoki Atari as collaborator and instigator.

All very dramatic, but nothing compared to what has happened in the last few hours. On this day, the whole of Paris, precious and precarious, infinitely delicate, is now vulnerable. One feels the open wound.

As I prepare myself to face the airport, with obvious new security measures, and a certainty of delay in being able to leave for the United States, I sit somberly, if briefly, with friends I have made in my past sojourns at this, my small hotel.

We are a sorry little group, each one of us in various stages of shock. I realize my mental listing of René's arrest successes as some sort of sop to the hollow feeling inside for what transpired last night in the bistros, on the streets, and in the concert hall and stadium. It is so hard to wrap one's mind and conscience around the brutality that occurred by men, who has Giscard reported to René, were 'laughing' as they sprayed the innocents with pellets of death.

"It's a new planet," Jean-Luc repeats.

"That well may be, old friend," I say, "but you will see that Paris and its people and those who love her will bring her down to earth again. It will happen. I know it."

Jean-Luc leans over and gives me a kiss, as I continue, "those with heart will always defeat the heartless."

CHAPTER 26

Paris – Tétanisée
(In Shock)

FRIDAY NIGHT, NOVEMBER 13th!

Saturday, the day after the night of the assassins, the streets are empty as Brit drives me to Charles de Gaulle airport to catch the plane taking me back to America. I expect a long delay in my departure, according to the radio reports, as a state of emergency has been declared by the President of France, as reported by, of all people, Monsieur Dupris. We can still hear the braying of police cars in the distance, the roar of ambulances, the sirens wailing. Brit and I are silent as the old Peugeot navigates the road.

I think of the bloody history of Paris – from the days when the Roman armies stormed the city, naming it Lutetia of the Parisii people, through the Huns invading, besieging Paris, the British kings attacking, seeking territory and power, and the Vikings, rowing down the Seine leaving a trail of blood in the water, through the Revolution, The Commune, two World Wars, the bombings around the Algerian conflict.

And, more recently, of course, *'Je suis Charlie'*.

Though the city may represent to many a sweet, bourgeois life, with elegant surroundings, brilliant museums, a glittering river, sumptuous *cuisine, yet,* above the cobblestoned streets and terraced *parcs,* it is a city of a people hardened by days and years of trauma.

Today is another such day - and just the beginning.

Ah, the empty streets. The wary glances. *Parisians* display a fierce realism, despite sadness and shock. There are few people. Those who are about, walk the streets pale and jittery.

The local bakers are open at dawn, even as the sirens still wail after the night of bloody horror. They open because they want to offer the homely, simple, familiar morning routine that the *Parisian* expects. The aroma of the classic *baguette,* the *croissant,* the *pain au chocolat,* oh, how they reassure and soothe the jumpy stomach, and a heart aching for the City of Light. As Al Jolson sang in the lovely Irving Berlin song, back in 1949, right after the cruel Nazi occupation, "Paris Wakes Up and Smiles".

This 'day-after', in mid-November, 2015, it tries to smile once more. But it's hard. Glass on the street, shattered into shards – like the bellboys in Jean-Luc's office – scattered in disarray. Broken lives. Lives in pieces. Lives no more. Ah Paris. My Paris. It will smile again because it is indestructible, and I know Paris will endure. After all, the ages have proved its legacy, the city's resilience - that no evil, however cruel, can overcome its beauty and its strength.

People everywhere are buying flowers, white roses – to place outside the stricken bistros, at the stadium entrance, on the street before the silenced concert hall, at the feet of Marianne, the embodiment of the French Republic, a 31-foot bronze statue in the center of La Place de République, near which Sue and I so recently had lunch.

Paris, the city of romance is challenged again, but the romance, the delight in it, is not forgotten. Never! *Parisians* live the past in the present, and yet the future beckons, and here, where enlightenment was born, where the Western world began, the city's life force will evoke an even greater passion to live a life of joy. Paris promises to smile again.

Sitting next to Brit in his little Peugeot, I realize he looks a little older, this big man with tousled hair. At a traffic stop, I suddenly reach up to touch his cheek and kiss him on the lips with passion. I can't help myself. Even in the city that produced Rodin's famous marble sculpture, "The Kiss", I am surprised by my own gesture.

I smile shyly at strangers in passing cars who catch my eye. I know this kiss is special. With all its tenderness, it validates life in the face of the barbarities, the hail of bullets that took place last night, worst of all, at the concert hall where Giscard Poignal happened to be. The restaurants, *Le Petit Cambodge* and *Le Belle Équipe* and others, and the *Stade de France* where attackers blew themselves up, were also among the sites of horror last night. Yet today, with this kiss, I celebrate life, my love for my partner, and for still being enclosed in the sweet embrace of the City of Light. Paris.

As we leave the metropolitan environs for the highway to the airport, as I look wistfully through the automobile window, I notice on a street corner, a somber, young father, clutching a small boy's hand. Each of them carries, in his other hand, a long, warm *baguette*. The symbolism of this quick image is unforgettable.

I'll be back to see Paris smile again, to kiss my lover, to taste again the crusty bread, the *oeuf en gelée*, the *boeuf bourguignon*, and the good red wine. They say, this menu could facilitate diplomatic breakthroughs! Perhaps so, but it will also please the palate and make one know one is in one's own skin, with the right person, at exactly the right time.

And in exactly the right place! Paris.

RECIPES FOR THE EMOTIONS
A BAKER'S DOZEN

Each of the following recipes refers to a moment of emotion in the body
of this book that complements the sensibilities of a special instance
of importance. Every one provides a culinary experience to match
what is going on in the mind and heart of he who eats, consumes,
with hunger, lust, anger, or love, the dish before him. (Or her.)

POULET BONNE FEMME
A dish for lovers.

1 4 lb roaster chicken
3 Tb butter
½ cup each, sliced carrots, celery, onion
2 cups chicken broth
Salt, pepper,
1 cup *champagne*

Preheat oven to 325 degrees.

Massage breast of chicken with softened butter. Sprinkle with salt and pepper, inside and out. In casserole, *sauté* vegetables in remaining butter until tender. Place chicken atop. Pour in *champagne* and broth to cover ½ of chicken. Bring to simmer on top of stove. Cover the casserole and place in oven for 1 hour, 45 minutes.

The *Sauce Supreme:*
4 Tb butter
5 Tb flour 1 cup chicken cooking broth
More *champagne* to taste
1cup heavy cream
Salt, pepper

Make a *roux* by mixing butter and flour in saucepan, whisking in the broth, *champagne,* and the heavy cream – simmer 2 minutes adding more cream as necessary.

Place chicken on cutting board. Slice. On plate, spoon *Sauce Supreme* over each piece.

The simplicity of juicy chicken – both white and dark meat – bathed in an exquisitely delicate coating, is unsullied by mushrooms, shallots.

It is pure chicken in cream – and *champagne!*

What's not to love? And who?

HOMARD JEAN-LUC

A dish to appease anger in the cracking of the shells, at the same time it fills the need to chew the rich meat.

1 ½ lb lobster
1 cup dry white wine
1 quart water
Salt

Put lobster in boiling, salter water/wine, headfirst.
Cover. Boil 8 to 10 minutes.
Remove from water. Place on board. Using a heavy, sharp knife and a mallet or hammer, split the lobster from head to tail and crush the shells. With a nutcracker, crack the claws.
(This is a great exercise for the *chef* who is angry!)

Serve with hot, melted butter, a *baguette,* and a fine white wine or *champagne.*

If the lobster is served to the diner whole, be sure to provide a mallet, nutcracker and tiny fork to extract the meat, after he/she has ripped the lobster apart.

(This is also a great excuse if the diner happens to be angry too. After the ritual of dismembering the lobster, its rich meat is unusually satisfying to the tooth!)

Should one prefer a more civilized dish, extract the lobster meat from the shells. In a copper *sauté* pan, melt 3 tablespoons of butter, stir in the lobster pieces, plus a good dollop of heavy cream, add a ½ cup of fine *cognac*, ignite the dish, and when the flames die, serve with a warm *baguette* and *champagne*.

Wow!

MUSHROOM *OMELETTE* TO DIE FOR

Be sure the mushrooms are pristine!

Preheat oven to 400 degrees

4 eggs, separated
2 Tb butter
Salt, pepper
4 Tb light cream
Beat yolks with the milk, salt and pepper.
Beat egg whites until stiff, and fold into the yolks gently.

½ lb sliced mushrooms
2 Tb butter
½ cup white wine
6 Tb heavy cream
Salt

Sauté mushrooms in butter. When slightly browned and dry, add salt, wine, and heavy cream. Simmer until slightly thickened.

In separate *sauté* pan, melt 2 tablespoons butter. Add egg mixture. Cook slowly until *omelette* is puffed up and slightly brown on top. Place mushrooms in cream over top and put *sauté* pan into oven for 8 minutes.

Cut into two wedges and serve.
(¼ cup *Gruyère* cheese can be added to the egg mixture, if desired, and 2 tbs. cheese sprinkled on top of mushrooms for final cooking.)

Avoid 'Jack-O-Lantern' mushrooms that resemble *Chanterelles*. Avoid 'Thimble *morels*'.

These can cause intense distress.
Or worse!

SOUPE A L'OIGNON

Simplicity for the soul.

3Tb butter
1 Tb olive oil
6 cups thinly sliced yellow onions
Salt
½ tsp sugar
Cook onions for 30 minutes in butter/oil or until caramelized and golden
brown.
Add 3 Tb flour
Stir into the onions for 3 minutes. Then add:

2 qts. hot beef bouillon
1 cup burgundy wine
2 bay leaves
1 tsp sage
Salt, pepper to taste
Simmer 40 minutes. Add ¼ cup *cognac* to soup.
Ladle soup into individual small casseroles.

1 *baguette* cut into ¾ inch slices. Paint each with butter and toast lightly. Pack one slice (or more) on each casserole.

1½ cups grated *Gruyère* and Parmesan, mixed.

Spread on the toasted bread, covering completely, sprinkle each with olive oil.

Bake in 350 degree oven for 30 minutes until cheese is melted and soup is bubbling hot.

How satisfying to the soul! And what a traditional and restorative answer to a hangover!

ENDIVE, PEAR, *ROQUEFORT* CHEESE, WALNUTS *SALADE VINAIGRETTE*

Because of its textures, and variety of flavor, this simple salad is an excellent pre-shopping experience. It opens the mind to explore new possibilities and accept fresh vision.

1 ripe Riviera pear, peeled and sliced into wedges
2 endive
¼ lb crumbled *Roquefort* cheese
A handful of halved walnuts

Vinaigrette
¼ cup good olive oil
Juice of 2 lemons
1 Tb Dijon mustard
Salt, pepper
Mix well.

Dress the endive with the *vinaigrette*. Place pears on endive leaves, top with *Roquefort* crumbles and walnuts. Drizzle remaining *vinaigrette* over all, if desired. This is a sparkling luncheon dish that peps up the appetite and prepares one for inspired shopping. Don't know exactly why, but it's true.

PIG'S FOOT AND A BOTTLE OF BEER

If this doesn't cure depression, I don't know what does!

Pigs' feet
Make a court bouillon:

1 bottle of beer	Bay leaf
2 Carrots	Parsley sprigs
2 cloves garlic	Salt and pepper
1 tsp thyme	2 quarts water

Have butcher cut pigs' feet long. Clean carefully.
Combine ingredients for court bouillon – let boil 30 minutes. Cool.
Simmer pig's feet 3-4 hours.
Cool.
Rub pork fat, chicken fat (both rendered) or butter, mixed with mustard, over pig's feet. Coat with dry bread crumbs. Grill under the broiler 5 inches from heat or roast in a hot oven (475 degrees) for 10-15 minutes.

Serve with a spicy sauce, (Heinz Chili Sauce mixed with horseradish, or *sauce diable*), more mustard, and pickles. And don't forget an ice-cold beer!

BOEUF BOURGUIGNON

A peasant's dish made elegant.

3 lb beef round cut into 2 inch pieces
6 oz bacon, diced
Olive oil
Salt, pepper
3 cups good burgundy wine
2 cups beef bouillon 1 lb mushrooms
2 cloves mashed garlic 18 small white onions
2 Tb tomato paste Butter, oil
Thyme, bay leaf Salt, pepper

3 Tb soft butter
3 Tb flour – to thicken sauce

Cook the bacon until lightly browned in a skillet. Remove. Salt and
pepper beef chunks. In bacon fat, *sauté* the meat, and as browned, place
in casserole.

Pour fat from skillet, deglaze with wine and pour into casserole with
bouillon, garlic, tomato paste, herbs and bacon bits.

Stir. Cover. Place in a 325 degree oven for 2 ½ to 3 hours.

While beef is cooking, slice mushrooms and *sauté* in oil and butter, salt and pepper. Peel onions and boil gently for 20 minutes.

When beef is tender, remove one cup of liquid, cream together the flour and butter and mix with the beef cooking liquid until smooth. Return mixture to casserole and stir into sauce. Add vegetables. Reheat gently on top of stove.

Although somewhat labor intensive, it's worth it!

COQ AU RIESLING

An ambrosial treatment of chicken.

1 chicken cut in eighths
2 Tb olive oil
2 Tb butter
Salt, pepper
1 lb mushrooms cut in thin slices
1 small clove garlic
1 ½ cups Riesling wine
1 Tb fresh thyme leaves
1 Tb flour
½ cup cognac
½ cup heavy cream

Salt, pepper the chicken pieces. Brown them skin side down in oil and butter in a Dutch oven. Remove. Add finely minced garlic to the pot. When slightly colored add ¼ cup of cognac to deglaze the pan. Brown the mushrooms in the pot, then add wine. Bring to a boil. Return chicken pieces to the pot with the juices, sprinkle with thyme leaves, cover and simmer over low heat for approximately 45 minutes.

Remove chicken to a platter. In ½ cup of sauce, mix flour and whisk it back into sauce. Add remaining cognac and the heavy cream, raising the heat so the sauce thickens slightly. Pour the sauce over the chicken – serve some on the side.

Although this dish is similar in ways to the *POULET BONNE FEMME*, its taste is more delicate, more light-hearted. It deserves to be served to best friends on a frosty night in a *château* in France – if possible.

SHORTBREAD COOKIES

To give to an injured one, by the remorseful, apologetic offender: just to say 'sorry.' Consumption of the sweet, buttery goodness can only bring forgiveness and a kiss.

3 sticks softened butter
¾ cups sugar
Cream together until fluffy
1½ tsp vanilla
3 cups flour
Add and mix well.
Roll dough into three rolls. Dough will be soft so shape carefully. Wrap in plastic wrap and refrigerate until dough is cold enough to slice, (at least a couple of hours).
Preheat oven to 350 degrees.
Slice dough into one-third- inch squares or rounds.
Place on cookie sheet evenly.
Bake 10-13 minutes until just golden around edges.
Remove and sprinkle with sugar.
Approx. 24 cookies per roll

The simplicity of these treats is matchless for soothing the injured spirit.

OSSOBUCO

Provide tiny spoons to extract the delicate interior of the shank bone. The marrow is exquisite.

4 veal shank bones ½ cup white wine
4 Tb olive oil ½ cup tomato puree
Flour to coat Chicken broth
Salt, pepper 1 anchovy fillet
1 clove mashed garlic

Parsley, grated lemon peel

Salt and pepper the flour and dredge the shanks. *Sauté* in olive oil until nicely browned. Add garlic, wine, anchovy fillet, and tomato puree to pan, plus enough chicken broth to come up to ½ the height of the meat. Cover and simmer (or place in oven at 350 degrees) for 1 hour.

When tender, add grated lemon peel and fresh parsley to the pan, stirring, and serve.

This is a delicate, elegant dish, surprisingly hearty and heartfelt.

POACHED PEARS

A light finish to a rich meal that leaves one feeling refreshed and satisfied.

4 Anjou pears – wash but do not peel
4 cloves – put clove in each pear

Syrup:
1 cup brown sugar
¾ cup water
Large pinch of cinnamon
Boil 5 minutes

Place pears upright in baking dish. Pour syrup over all and bake at 350 degrees for 25 minutes or until tender, basting occasionally.

Add ½ cup *cognac*

Serve hot with *crème fraiche* – or cold with a wedge of cheese –Gorgonzola is most piquant as accompaniment.

POMME DE TERRE AU CAVIAR

This is the answer to absolutely everything! The ultimate comfort food.

1 large baking potato
2 Tb butter
2 Tb sour cream
Salt, pepper
Caviar or salmon roe – the best, and as much as possible
Meyer lemon wedge

Wash and bake potato in oven at 400 degrees.
When done (about 50 minutes), carefully split the potato at the top, press the flesh upward and put softened butter, salt and pepper into the interior, fluffing the potato, adding sour cream as you do so. The mixture should be light and smooth. At table, serve the potato with a side dish of caviar, and a plate with more butter and sour cream.

Place the caviar or salmon roe (equally good) on top of the potato, with a squirt of lemon juice (optional) and prepare to savor this most delightful of all combinations. Of course, you will want to add more caviar as you progress. And more butter. And more sour cream. Eat slowly!

SOUFFLÉ

In all its variations, a soufflé, from sweet to savory, or imbued with a favorite liqueur, is always light and cheerful to behold, giving one the promise of options to choose from and a future to be enjoyed.

The simplest base:
3 Tb butter 4 eggs separated
3 Tb flour 1 extra egg white
1 cup milk

In pan melt butter, blend in flour, gradually stir in milk to make a white sauce. Cool slightly.

***At this point add **Flavorings** and mix.

Beat 4 egg yolks until lemon-colored. Whip 5 egg whites until stiff. Carefully, slowly stir white sauce and yolks together (…the yolks are hot, so proceed gently). When combined, fold in beaten whites. Place into a greased *soufflé* dish and bake in a 375 degree oven for 35 minutes.

*****Flavorings** – depending on one's mood. The following are suggestions for Savory, Sweet and Spirited Soufflé's.

SAVORY:

1 cup Parmesan, or *Gruyère*, or Cheddar, or *Roquefort*

Dash Worcestershire sauce

1 cup spinach, or broccoli - finely chopped – add 1 Tb flour in white sauce - tsp salt

1 can minced clams – use can liquid with milk to make 1 cup in preparing white sauce -Dash lemon juice

SWEET:

2 squares semisweet chocolate melted with ¼ cup sugar

3 Tb lemon juice, 1 Tb grated lemon rind, sugar to taste
Serve hot or cold with whipped cream.

3 Tb Orange juice, 1 Tb grated orange rind, sugar to taste
Serve hot or cold with whipped cream.

1 cup raspberry, strawberry, peach, or other fruit puree –sugar to taste
Serve hot or cold with whipped cream.

SPIRITED:

*Quarter cup Liqueur –*Armagnac, Cognac, Grand Marnier, Chartreuse*
Whatever one desires!
Add 1 extra Tb flour in white sauce. Add ¼ cup sugar when beating egg yolks.

*This last *soufflé* will surely raise the spirits, particularly if served with an additional snifter of liqueur and a black espresso!

AUTHOR'S COMMENT

If it seems that recipes here – listed to match emotions in the text – contain quantities of butter and cream and spirits of various kinds, herbs, more butter and *champagne* and *cognac,* sour cream and yes, caviar, it is obviously true.

Yet all these additions only contribute a *richesse* to whatever is on or in the stove. They provide *une friandise extraordinaire* (an extraordinary appreciation of food) to the lucky one who partakes of the sublime dishes.

They are the extra step. They are the secret touch. They are essential. Do not leave any of these embellishments out!

Although the recipes included are derivative of recipes of master *chefs,* such as Julia Child, James Beard, Ina Garten, they are NOT direct copies, but include certain little tricks of my own.

While the last recipe for *soufflé* is nowhere in the body of the book, I felt it an elegant addition to the culinary experience.

Mon Appétit!

Printed in the United States
By Bookmasters